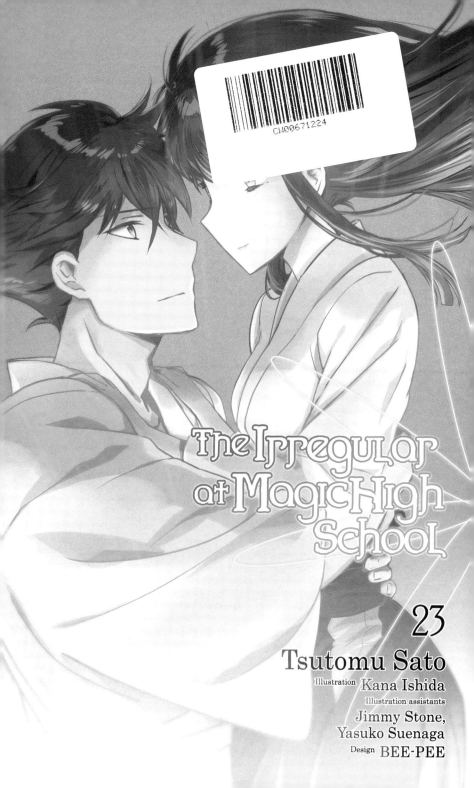

The Irregular at Magic High School

23

Tsutomu Sato

Illustration **Kana Ishida**

Illustration assistants

Jimmy Stone,
Yasuko Suenaga

Design **BEE-PEE**

The Dione Project

The Dione Project is an international grand space development project helmed by the USNA's National Science Agency (NSA) engineer Edward Clark. Its goal is to use magicians and magic technology to terraform Venus with resources from the Jupiter region.

The diameter of Venus is 0.95 times that of the Earth's, and its gravity is 0.9 times that of the Earth's. In this respect, Venus is a more suitable destination for human settlement than Mars. However, Venus's thick carbon dioxide atmosphere, sulfuric acid clouds, and high temperatures, which appear to be caused by a greenhouse effect, make it difficult to modify the planet's environment.

The ultimate purpose of the project is to use magic technology to permanently alter the atmosphere of Venus, which is an extreme challenge for conventional technology alone.

The Four Schema of the Dione Project

① Weighting- and acceleration-type magic will be used to launch materials and prefabricated production plants from Earth's surface into space. The most significant challenge when constructing large-scale structures in space is overcoming Earth's gravity. For that reason, the project will employ magically augmented rockets to transport large masses into space.

② Magicians will mine the asteroid belt for the metals needed for the project. The use of movement magic will solve the propellant problem while mining in a zero-gravity environment.

③ Magic will be employed to extract hydrogen from Jupiter and transport it to Venus. The Sabatier reaction, which produces methane and water when hydrogen reacts with carbon dioxide under high temperature and high pressure, will help introduce water to Venus, a currently dry environment, and simultaneously reduce carbon dioxide emissions. Nickel mined in ① will be used as a catalyst for the reaction.

④ To counter the effects mentioned in ③, which includes Venus being surrounded by more potent greenhouse gases than carbon dioxide (e.g., water vapor and methane), large blocks of ice will be extracted from one of Jupiter's Galilean moons, Callisto. Magic will then be used to transport this ice and launch it into Venus's atmosphere to lower the planet's temperature.

The Status of Space Development as of 2097

Space development remains stagnant since its interruption by social turmoil caused by global cooling and subsequent war. Ability to conduct manned spaceflight has likewise declined since the beginning of the twenty-first century.

A Comment from Igor Andreivich Bezobrazov on His Participation in the Project

"I believe the terraforming of Venus holds a significance that transcends international squabbles. For over a century, humanity has been haunted by the looming danger of overpopulation. This fear could lead to catastrophic conflicts and an irreversible decline in our civilization's dynamism in the not too distant future. Securing more habitats for humanity is perhaps the only solution to the impending crisis that threatens our future."

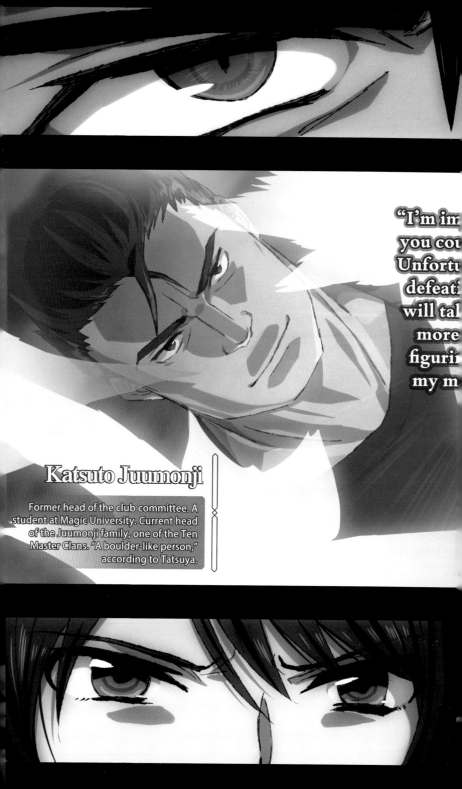

"I'm im
you co
Unfortu
defeat
will tal
more
figuri
my m

Katsuto Juumonji

Former head of the club committee. A
student at Magic University. Current head
of the Juumonji family, one of the Ten
Master Clans. "A boulder-like person,"
according to Tatsuya.

"Is that an Area-Interference-Information-Boosting Expansion Wall?"

Tatsuya Shiba

Miyuki's older brother. In Class 3-E at First High. Approaches everything in a detached manner, except his role as Miyuki's Guardian.

Angelina Kudou Shields

Entered Magic High School two years
ago under the guise of an exchange
student. A blond, blue-eyed beauty with
exceptional magical skills. In reality, she
goes by Major Angie Sirius, the USNA
Army's strongest magician and a member
of the Thirteen Apostles.

"Tatsuya?"

The Irregular at MagicHigh School

ISOLATION ARC

23

Tsutomu Sato

Illustration Kana Ishida

YEN ON

NEW YORK

THE IRREGULAR AT MAGIC HIGH SCHOOL
TSUTOMU SATO

Translation by Kenia A. Hara
Cover art by Kana Ishida

MAHOUKA KOUKOU NO RETTOUSEI Vol. 23
©Tsutomu Sato 2017
Edited by Dengeki Bunko
First published in Japan in 2017 by KADOKAWA CORPORATION, Tokyo.
English translation rights arranged with KADOKAWA CORPORATION, Tokyo, through Tuttle-Mori Agency, Inc., Tokyo.

English translation © 2024 by Yen Press, LLC

Yen On
150 West 30th Street, 19th Floor
New York, NY 10001

Visit us at yenpress.com
facebook.com/yenpress
twitter.com/yenpress
yenpress.tumblr.com
instagram.com/yenpress

First Yen On Edition: September 2024
Edited by Yen On Editorial: Ivan Liang
Designed by Yen Press Design: Wendy Chan

Library of Congress Cataloging-in-Publication Data
Names: Sato, Tsutomu. | Ishida, Kana, illustrator.
Title: The irregular at Magic High School / Tsutomu Sato ; Illustrations by Kana Ishida.
Other titles: Mahōka kōkō no rettosei. English
Description: First Yen On edition. | New York, NY : Yen On, 2016–
Identifiers: LCCN 2015042401 | ISBN 9780316348805 (v 1 : pbk.)
Subjects: CYAC: Brothers and sisters—Fiction. | Magic—Fiction. | High schools—Fiction. | Schools—Fiction. | Japan—Fiction. | Science fiction.
Classification: LCC PZ7.1.S265 Ir 2016 | DDC [Fic]—dc23
LC record available at http://lccn.loc.gov/2015042401

ISBNs: 978-1-9753-4522-8 (paperback)
        978-1-9753-4523-5 (ebook)

10 9 8 7 6 5 4 3 2 1

LSC-C

Printed in the United States of America

The Irregular at MagicHigh School

ISOLATION ARC

An irregular older brother with a certain flaw.
An honor roll younger sister who is perfectly flawless.

When the two siblings enrolled in Magic High School,
a dramatic life unfolded—

Character

Tatsuya Shiba

Class 3-E.
Approaches everything in a detached manner. His sister Miyuki's Guardian.

Miyuki Shiba

Class 3-A. Tatsuya's younger sister; enrolled as the top student last year. Specializes in freezing magic. Dotes on her older brother.

Leonhard Saijou

Class 3-F. Tatsuya's friend. Course 2 student. Specializes in hardening magic. Has a cheerful personality.

Erika Chiba

Class 3-F. Tatsuya's friend. Course 2 student. A charming troublemaker.

Mizuki Shibata

Class 3-E. Tatsuya's friend. Has pushion-radiation sensitivity. Serious and a bit of an airhead.

Mikihiko Yoshida

Class 3-B. From a famous family that uses old magic. Has known Erika since they were children.

Honoka Mitsui

Class 3-A. Miyuki's classmate. Specializes in light-wave vibration magic. Impulsive when emotional.

Shizuku Kitayama

Class 3-A. Miyuki's classmate. Specializes in vibration and acceleration magic. Doesn't show emotional ups and downs very much.

Subaru Satomi

Class 3-D. Frequently mistaken for a pretty boy. Cheerful and easy to get along with.

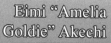

Eimi "Amelia Goldie" Akechi

Class 3-B. A quarter Japanese. Almost everyone calls her "Amy." Daughter of the prominent Goldie family.

Akaha Sakurakouji

Class 3-B. Friends with Subaru and Amy. Wears gothic lolita clothes and loves theme parks.

Shun Morisaki

Class 3-A. Miyuki's classmate. Specializes in CAD quick-draw. Takes great pride in being a Course 1 student.

Hagane Tomitsuka

Class 3-E. A magic martial arts user with the nickname "Range Zero."

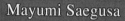

Mayumi Saegusa

An alum. Currently attends Magic University. Has a devilish personality but weak when on the defensive.

Azusa Nakajou

An alum. Former student council president. Shy and has trouble expressing herself.

Suzune Ichihara

An alum. Currently a student at Magic University. Calm, collected, and book smart.

Hanzou Gyoubu-Shoujou Hattori

An alum. Former head of the club committee. Gifted but can be too serious at times.

Mari Watanabe

An alum. Mayumi's good friend. Well-rounded and often sporting for a fight.

Katsuto Juumonji

An alum. Currently a student at Magic University. "A boulder-like person," according to Tatsuya.

Koutarou Tatsumi

An alum and former member of the disciplinary committee. Has a heroic and dynamic personality.

Isao Sekimoto

An alum and former member of the disciplinary committee. Lost the Thesis Competition. Committed acts of espionage.

Midori Sawaki

An alum. Former member of the disciplinary committee. Has a complex about his girlish name.

Takeaki Kirihara

An alum. Junior High Kanto Kenjutsu Tournament champion.

Kei Isori

An alum. Former student council treasurer. Excels in magical theory. Engaged to Kanon.

Sayaka Mibu

An alum. Placed second in the nation at the girl's Junior High Kendo Tournament.

Kanon Chiyoda

An alum. Former chairwoman of the disciplinary committee. As confrontational as her predecessor, Mari.

Kasumi Saegusa

A junior. Mayumi Saegusa's younger sister. Izumi's older twin sister. Has a cheerful and feisty personality.

Takuma Shippou

A junior. Eldest son of the Shippou family, one of the families with excellent magicians and a new addition to the Ten Master Clans.

Izumi Saegusa

A junior. Mayumi Saegusa's younger sister. Kasumi's younger twin sister. Has a meek and gentle personality.

Minami Sakurai

A junior. Presents herself as Tatsuya and Miyuki's cousin. A Guardian candidate for Miyuki.

Kento Sumisu

A junior. A Caucasian boy whose parents are naturalized Japanese citizens from the USNA.

Koharu Hirakawa

An alum. Participated as an engineer in the Nine School Competition. Withdrew from the Thesis Competition.

Chiaki Hirakawa

A senior. Holds enmity toward Tatsuya.

Shiina Mitsuya

A new student enrolled at First High. Always wears custom earmuffs due to her keen sense of hearing.

Saburou Yaguruma

Shiina's childhood friend and self-proclaimed bodyguard.

Haruka Ono

A general counselor of First High. Tends to get bullied but has another side to her personality.

Yakumo Kokonoe

A user of an ancient magic called *ninjutsu*. Tatsuya's martial arts master.

Satomi Asuka

First High nurse. Male students love her calm and warm smile.

Kazuo Tsuzura

First High teacher. Specializes in magic geometry. Manages the Thesis Competition team.

Jennifer Smith

A Caucasian woman naturalized as a Japanese citizen. Teaches Tatsuya's class and magic engineering classes.

Tomoko Chikura

An alum. Competed in the women's solo Shields Down, an event at the Nine School Competition.

Tsugumi Igarashi

An alum. Former biathlon club president.

Yousuke Igarashi

A senior. Tsugumi's younger brother. Has a somewhat reserved personality.

Kerry Minakami

An alum. Male representative for the main Monolith Code, an event at the Nine School Competition.

Kumiko Kunisaki

An alum. Amy's teammate in the Rower and Gunner event at the Nine School Competition. Has a frank personality.

Masaki Ichijou

A senior at Third High. Direct heir to the Ichijou family, one of the Ten Master Clans.

Gouki Ichijou

Masaki's father. Current head of the Ichijou family, one of the Ten Master Clans.

Shinkurou Kichijouji

A senior at Third High. Also known as Cardinal George.

Midori Ichijou

Masaki's mother. Warm and good at cooking.

Akane Ichijou

Eldest Ichijou daughter. Masaki's younger sister. A junior in middle school. Likes Shinkurou.

Ushio Kitayama

Shizuku's father. Big shot in the business world. His business name is Ushio Kitagata.

Ruri Ichijou

Second Ichijou daughter. Masaki's younger sister. A put-together girl who marches to the beat of her own drum.

Benio Kitayama

Shizuku's mother. An A-rank magician who was once renowned for her vibration magic.

Wataru Kitayama

Shizuku's younger brother. Just started middle school. Dearly loves his older sister. Aims to be a magic engineer.

Harumi Naruse

Shizuku's older cousin. Student at National Magic University Fourth Affiliated High School.

Pixie

A home helper robot belonging to Magic High School. Official name 3H (Humanoid Home Helper: a human-shaped chore-assisting robot) Type P94.

Ushiyama

Manager of Four Leaves Technology's CAD R&D Section 3. Has earned Tatsuya's trust.

Toshikazu Chiba

Erika Chiba's eldest brother. Deceased. Worked at the Ministry of Police.

Ernst Rosen

A prominent CAD manufacturer. President of Rosen Magicraft's Japanese branch.

Naotsugu Chiba

Erika Chiba's second-eldest brother. Mari's lover. Possesses full mastery of the Chiba (thousand blades) style of kenjutsu. Nicknamed "Kirin Child of the Chiba."

Retsu Kudou

Renowned as the strongest magician in the world. Given the honorary title of Sage.

Inagaki

Deceased. When he was alive, he worked as an inspector at the Ministry of Police and was Toshikazu Chiba's subordinate.

Makoto Kudou

Son of Retsu Kudou, elder of Japan's magic world, and current head of the Kudou family.

Anna Rosen Katori

Erika's mother. Half Japanese and half German, was the mistress of Erika's father, the current leader of the Chiba.

Minoru Kudou

Makoto's son. Second year at the National Magic University Second Affiliated High School, but barely attends due to frequent illness. Also Kyouko Fujibayashi's younger brother by a different father.

Mamoru Kuki

One of the Eighteen Support Clans. Follows the Kudou family. Calls Retsu Kudou "Sensei" out of respect.

Maki Sawamura

An impressive actress nominated as best female lead for distinguished film awards. Acknowledged for both her beauty and acting skills.

Harunobu Kazama

Commanding officer of the 101st Brigade's Independent Magic Battalion. Ranked lieutenant colonel.

Shigeru Sanada

Executive officer of the 101st Brigade's Independent Magic Battalion. Ranked major.

Kyouko Fujibayashi

Female officer serving as Kazama's aide. Ranked first lieutenant.

Hiromi Saeki

Commander of the Japan Ground Defense Force's 101st Brigade. Ranked major general. Superior officer to Harunobu Kazama, commanding officer of the Independent Magic Battalion. Due to her appearance, she is also known as the Silver Fox.

Muraji Yanagi

Executive officer of the 101st Brigade's Independent Magic Battalion. Ranked major.

Kousuke Yamanaka

Executive officer of the 101st Brigade's Independent Magic Battalion. Physician ranked major. First-rate healing magician.

Sakai

Belongs to the Japan Ground Defense Force's general headquarters. Ranked colonel. Seen as staunchly anti–Great Asian Alliance.

Xiangshan Chen

Leader of the Great Asian Alliance Army's Special Covert Forces. Has a heartless personality.

Ganghu Lu

The ace magician of the Great Asian Alliance Army's Special Covert Forces. Also known as the "Man-Eating Tiger."

Gongjin Zhou

A handsome young man who brought Lu and Chen to Yokohama. A mysterious figure who hangs around Chinatown.

Rin

A girl Morisaki saved. Her full name is Meiling Sun. The new leader of the Hong Kong–based international crime syndicate No-Head Dragon.

Bradley Chan

A deserter of the Great Asian Alliance. Ranked first lieutenant.

Daniel Liu

A deserter of the Great Asian Alliance, like Chan. Also one of the architects of the sabotage operation in Okinawa.

Joseph Higaki

A military magician who fought the Great Asian Alliance alongside Tatsuya during the previous invasion of Okinawa. One of the Leftover Blood—descendants of orphaned children of the American soldiers who had been stationed in Okinawa.

Maya Yotsuba

Tatsuya and Miyuki's aunt. Miya's younger twin sister. The current head of the Yotsuba.

Katsushige Shibata

Former candidate to become the next leader of the Yotsuba clan. Employed by the Ministry of Defense. An alum of Fifth High. Specializes in convergence magic.

Hayama

An elderly butler employed by Maya.

Kotona Tsutsumi

One of Katsushige Shibata's Guardians. A second-generation Bard series engineered magician. Specializes in sound-based magic.

Miya Shiba

Tatsuya and Miyuki's actual mother. Deceased. The only magician skilled in mental construction interference magic.

Kanata Tsutsumi

One of Katsushige Shibata's Guardians. A second-generation Bard series engineered magician. Like his older sister, Kotona, he specializes in sound-based magic.

Honami Sakurai

Miya's Guardian. Deceased. Part of the first generation of the Sakura series, engineered magicians with strengthened magical capacity through genetic modification.

Mitsugu Kuroba

Miya Shiba and Maya Yotsuba's cousin. Father of Ayako and Fumiya.

Sayuri Shiba

Tatsuya and Miyuki's stepmother. Dislikes them.

Ayako Kuroba

Tatsuya and Miyuki's second cousin. Has a younger twin brother named Fumiya. Student at Fourth High.

Yuuka Tsukuba

A candidate to become the next leader of the Yotsuba clan. Twenty-two years old. Former vice president of First High's student council. Currently a senior attending Magic University. Skilled at mental interference magic.

Fumiya Kuroba

Former candidate for the next head of the Yotsuba clan. Has an older twin sister named Ayako. Student at Fourth High.

Yoshimi

A Yotsuba magician related to the Kuroba. A psychometrist specializing in reading the psionic traces left behind in psionic information bodies. Very secretive.

Angelina Kudou Shields

Commander of the USNA's magician unit, the Stars. Ranked major. Nickname is Lina. Also one of the strategic magicians called the Thirteen Apostles.

Virginia Balance

The USNA Joint Chiefs of Staff Information Bureau Internal Inspection Office's first deputy commissioner. Ranked colonel. Went to Japan in order to support Lina.

Silvia Mercury First

A planet-class magician in the USNA's magician unit, the Stars. Ranked warrant officer. Nickname is Silvie. Code name is Mercury First. During a mission in Japan, she serves as Major Sirius's aide.

Benjamin Canopus

Number two in the USNA's magician unit, the Stars. Ranked major. Takes command when Major Sirius is absent.

Mikaela Hongou

An agent sent into Japan by the USNA (although she actually works as a magic scientist for the Department of Defense). Nicknamed Mia.

Claire

Hunter Q—a female soldier in the magician unit Stardust for those who don't make it as Stars. Q refers to the 17th pursuit unit.

Alfred Fomalhaut

A first-degree star magician in the USNA's magician unit, the Stars. Rank is first lieutenant. Nicknamed Freddie. Currently AWOL.

Rachel

Hunter R—a female soldier in the magician unit Stardust for those who don't make it as Stars. R refers to the 18th pursuit unit.

Charles Sullivan

A satellite-class magician in the USNA's magician unit, the Stars. Code name is Deimos Second. Currently AWOL.

Kanda

A young politician affiliated with the Civil Rights Party. Supporter of civil rights in opposition to the military. Also anti-magician.

Raymond S. Clark

A student at the high school in Berkeley, USNA, where Shizuku studies abroad. A Caucasian boy who wastes no time making advances on Shizuku. Secretly one of the Seven Sages.

Kouzuke

A young Tokyo-based politician in the ruling party. Known as a legislator with favorable views toward magicians.

Gu Jie

One of the Seven Sages.
Also known as Gide Hague.
A survivor of a Dahanese
military's mage unit.

Kazukiyo Oumi

Known as the Dollmaker, a magic researcher
who specializes in necromancy and a
practitioner of ancient magic. Rumored to
use forbidden magic to reanimate corpses.

Joe Du

A mysterious man aiding Gu Jie's escape from Japan. Skilled enough at his job to
consistently evade the Ten Master Clans magicians hunting them.

James Jackson

A tourist visiting Okinawa
from Australia. Actually a—

Karla Schmidt

A German Union strategic magician
and academic conducting research
at Berlin University.

Jasmine Jackson

James's daughter. She seems
no older than twelve but acts
mature for her age.

Igor Andreivich Bezobrazov

A strategic magician of the
New Soviet Union and leading
magic researcher at the
Science Academy.

William MacLeod

A British strategic magician.
A prodigy who has earned
several teaching accolades
from universities abroad.

Edward Clark

An engineer working for
the USNA National Science
Agency (NSA). Administrator
of Hlidskjalf.

Mai Futatsugi

Head of the Futatsugi clan, one of the Ten Master Clans. Resides in Ashiya in Hyogo Prefecture. Publicly the majority shareholder in a variety of industrial chemical- and food-processing companies. Responsible for the Hanshin and Chugoku regions.

Kouichi Saegusa

Mayumi's father and current leader of the Saegusa clan. An ultra-top-class magician.

Saburou Nakura

A powerful magician employed by the Saegusa family. Mainly serves as Mayumi's personal bodyguard.

Gen Mitsuya

Head of the Mitsuya clan, one of the Ten Master Clans. Resides in Atsugi in Kanagawa Prefecture. While it isn't exactly public knowledge, he works as an international small arms broker. Manages Lab Three, which is still operational to this day.

Isami Itsuwa

Head of the Itsuwa clan, one of the Ten Master Clans. Resides in Uwajima in Ehime Prefecture. Publicly the executive and owner of a marine-shipping company. Responsible for the Tokai, Gifu, and Nagano regions.

Atsuko Mutsuzuka

Head of the Mutsuzuka clan, one of the Ten Master Clans. Resides in Sendai in Miyagi Prefecture. Publicly the owner of a geothermal energy exploration company. Responsible for the Tohoku region.

Raizou Yatsushiro

Head of the Yatsushiro clan, one of the Ten Master Clans. Resides in Fukuoka Prefecture. Publicly a university lecturer and majority shareholder in several telecommunications companies. Responsible for all of the Kyushu region, minus Okinawa.

Kazuki Juumonji

Former head of the Juumonji clan, one of the Ten Master Clans. Resides in Tokyo. Publicly the owner of a civil engineering and construction company that primarily serves the armed forces. Shares responsibility for the Kanto region, including Izu, with the Saegusa family.

Aoba Toudou

Yakumo refers to him as His Excellency, Priest Seiha. An old man with the shaved head of a priest, his origin and past are unknown. Per Yakumo, he appears to be a sponsor of the Yotsuba clan.

Tsukasa Tooyama

A member of the Tooyama clan, one of the Eighteen Support Clans, which aids the Ten Master Clans. The Tooyama exist to protect the functions of the state rather than the people.

Glossary

Course 1 student emblem

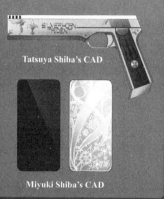

Tatsuya Shiba's CAD

Miyuki Shiba's CAD

Magic High School

Nickname for the high schools affiliated with the National Magic University. There are nine schools throughout the nation. First High to Third High adopt a system that splits its two hundred incoming freshmen into Course 1 and Course 2 students.

Blooms, Weeds

Slang terms used at First High to express the gap between Course 1 and Course 2 students. Course 1 student uniforms sport an eight-petaled emblem on the left breast, while Course 2 student uniforms do not.

CAD (Casting Assistant Device)

A device that simplifies magic casting. Magical programming is recorded within. There are many types and forms, some specialized and others multipurpose.

Four Leaves Technology (FLT)

A domestic CAD manufacturer. Originally more famous for magical-product engineering than for developing finished products, the development of the Silver model has made FLT much more widely known in their industry.

Taurus Silver

A genius engineer said to have advanced specialized CAD software by a decade in the span of a single year.

Eidos (individual information bodies)

Originally a term from Greek philosophy. In modern magic, eidos refers to the information bodies that accompany events. They form a so-called record of those events existing in the world, and can be considered the footprints of an object's state of being in the universe, be that active or passive. The definition of magic in its modern form is that of a technology that alters events by altering the information bodies composing them.

Idea (information body dimension)

Originally a term from Greek philosophy, pronounced "ee-dee-ah." In modern magic, Idea refers to the platform upon which eidos, or information bodies, are recorded. The primary function of magic is to yield a magic program (a spell sequence) on this Idea medium and overwrite the eidos recorded there.

Activation sequence

The blueprints of magic—and the programming that constructs it. Activation sequences are stored within CADs in a compressed format. Magicians send psionic waves into the CAD, which then expands the data and uses it to convert the activation sequence into a signal. This signal returns to the magician with the decompressed magic program.

Psions (thought particles)

Massless particles belonging to the dimension of spiritual phenomena. These information particles record products of awareness and thought. Eidos are considered the theoretical basis for modern magic, while activation sequences and magic programs are the technology forming its practical basis. All three of these bodies of information are made of psions.

Pushions (spirit particles)

Massless particles belonging to the dimension of spiritual phenomena. Their existence has been confirmed, but their true form and function have yet to be determined. In general, magicians are only able to sense energized pushions.

Magician

An abbreviation of magic technician. Refers to those with the skills to use magic at a practical level.

Magic program

An information body used to temporarily alter information connected to events. Constructed from psions possessed by magicians. Sometimes shortened to magigram.

Magic-calculation region

A mental region that constructs magic programs. The essential core of the talent of magic. Exists within the magician's unconscious regions. Though magicians can normally consciously use the magic-calculation region, they cannot perceive the processing happening within. The magic-calculation region may be called a black box, even for the magician performing the task.

Magic program output process

1. An activation sequence is transmitted to a CAD. This is called "reading an activation sequence."
2. Variables are added to the activation sequence and sent to the magic-calculation region.
3. A magic program is constructed from the activation sequence and its variables.
4. The constructed magic program is sent along the "route" from the highest part of the unconscious mind to the lowest part of the conscious mind, out the "gate" between consciousness and unconsciousness, and output to the Idea.
5. The magic program output interferes with the eidos at designated coordinates and overwrites them.

   With a single-type, single-process spell, this five-stage process can be completed in under half a second. This is the bar for practical-level use with magicians.

Magic evaluation standards

The speed with which a magician constructs psionic information bodies is known as magical throughput, or processing speed. The scale and scope of the information bodies magicians can construct is known as magical capacity. The strength with which magicians overwrite eidos with magic programs is known as magical power.

Cardinal Code hypothesis

A school of thought claiming there is the existence of a total of sixteen foundational plus and minus magic programs within the eight types of magic—acceleration, weighting, movement, vibration, convergence, dispersion, absorption, and emission.

Typed magic

Any magic belonging to the four families and eight types.

Exotyped magic

A term for spells that control mental phenomena rather than physical ones. Encompasses many fields, from divine magic and spirit magic—which employs spiritual presences—to mind reading, astral form separation, and consciousness control.

Ten Master Clans

The most powerful magician organization in Japan. The ten families are chosen every four years from among the following twenty-eight families: Ichijou, Ichinokura, Isshiki, Futatsugi, Nikaidou, Nihei, Mitsuya, Mikazuki, Yotsuba, Itsuwa, Gotou, Itsumi, Mutsuzuka, Rokkaku, Rokugou, Roppongi, Saegusa, Shippou, Tanabata, Nanase, Yatsushiro, Hassaku, Hachiman, Kudou, Kuki, Kuzumi, Juumonji, and Tooyama.

Numbers

Just like how the Ten Master Clans contain a number from one to ten in their surnames, well-known families within the Hundred Families use numbers eleven or greater, such as Chiyoda (one thousand), Isori (fifty), and Chiba (one thousand). Although the number value is not equivalent to the family's level of strength, the presence of a number in a surname is a broad indication of that family's prominent lineage and talent.

Non-numbers

Also called Extra Numbers, or simply Extras. Magician families who have been stripped of their number. Back in the day when magicians were used as weapons and experimental subjects, success cases were given numbers, while failures—those who did not produce sufficient results—were not.

Various Spells

• Cocytus

Exotyped magic that freezes the mind. A frozen mind cannot order the flesh to die, so anyone subject to this spell enters a state of mental and physical stasis.

• Rumbling

An old spell that vibrates the ground to create a medium for an independent information body known as a spirit.

• Program Dispersion

A spell that dismantles a magic program, the main component of a spell, into a group of psionic particles with no meaningful structure. Since magic programs affect the information bodies associated with events, it is necessary for the information structure to be exposed, leaving no way to prevent interference against the magic program itself.

• Program Demolition

A typeless spell that rams a mass of compressed psionic particles directly into an object without passing through the Idea, causing it to explode and blow away the psionic information bodies recorded in magic, such as activation sequences and magic programs. Although this spell is considered a type of magic because it is a psionic bullet without any structure such as a magic program for altering events, it is not affected by Information Boost or Area Interface. The pressure of the bullet itself also repels any Cast Jamming effects. Since it has zero physical effect, it is unblockable.

• Mine Origin

A spell that imparts strong vibrations to anything that can be conceptualized as the ground—including dirt, boulders, sand, and concrete—regardless of its composition.

• Fissure

A spell that uses independent information bodies or spirits as a medium to push a line into the ground and create a fissure in the earth.

• Dry Blizzard

A spell that gathers carbon dioxide from the air, creates dry-ice particles, then converts the extra heat energy from the freezing process to kinetic energy to launch the dry-ice particles at a high speed.

• Slithering Thunders

In addition to condensing the water vapor from Dry Blizzard's dry-ice evaporation and creating a highly conductive mist with the evaporated carbon dioxide in it, this spell creates static electricity with vibration-type magic and emission-type magic. A combination spell, it also fires an electric attack at an enemy using the carbon gas-filled mist and water droplets as a conductor.

• Niflheim

A vibration- and deceleration-type area-of-effect spell. It chills a large volume of air, then moves it to freeze a wide range. In blunt terms, it creates a super-large refrigerator. The white mist that appears upon activation is the particles of frozen ice and dry ice, but at higher levels, a mist of frozen liquid nitrogen occurs.

• Burst

A dispersion-type spell that vaporizes the liquid inside a target object. When used on a creature, the spell will vaporize bodily fluids and cause the body to rupture. When used on a machine powered by internal combustion, the spell vaporizes the fuel and makes it explode. Fuel cells see the same result, and even if no combustible fuel is on board, there is no machine that does not contain some liquid, such as battery fluid, hydraulic fluid, coolant, or lubricant; once Burst activates, virtually any machine will be destroyed.

• Disheveled Hair

An old spell that, instead of specifying a direction and changing the wind's direction to that, uses air current control to bring about the vague result of "tangling" it, causing currents along the ground that entangle an opponent's feet in the grass. Only usable on plains with grass of a certain height.

Magic Swords

Aside from fighting techniques that use magic itself as a weapon, another method of magical combat involves techniques for using magic to strengthen and control weapons. The majority of these spells combine magic with projectile weapons such as guns and bows, but the art of the sword, known as kenjutsu, has developed in Japan as well as a way to link magic with sword techniques. This has led to magic technicians formulating personal-use magic techniques known as magic swords, which can be said to be both modern and ancient magic.

1. High-Frequency Blade

A spell that locally liquefies a solid body and cleaves it by causing a blade to vibrate at a high speed, then propagate the vibration that exceeds the molecular cohesive force of matter it comes in contact with. Used as a set with a spell to prevent the blade from breaking.

2. Pressure Cut

A spell that generates left-right perpendicular repulsive force relative to the angle of a slashing blade edge, causing the blade to force apart any object it touches and thereby cleave it. The size of the repulsive field is less than a millimeter, but it has the strength to interfere with light, so when seen from the front, the blade edge becomes a black line.

3. Douji-Giri (Simultaneous Cut)

An ancient magic spell passed down as a secret sword art of the Genji. It is a magic sword technique wherein the user remotely manipulates two blades through a third in their hands in order to have the swords surround an opponent and slash simultaneously. *Douji* is the Japanese pronunciation for both "simultaneous" and "child," so this ambiguity was used to keep the inherited nature of the technique a secret.

4. Zantetsu (Iron Cleaver)

A secret sword art of the Chiba clan. Rather than defining a katana as a hulk of steel and iron, this movement spell defines it as a single concept, then the spell moves the katana along a slashing path set by the magic program. The result is that the katana is defined as a mono-molecular blade, never breaking, bending, or chipping as it slices through any objects in its path.

5. Jinrai Zantetsu (Lightning Iron Cleaver)

An expanded version of Zantetsu that makes use of the Ikazuchi-Maru, a personal-armament device. By defining the katana and its wielder as one collective concept, the spell executes the entire series of actions, from enemy contact to slash, incredibly quickly and with faultless precision.

6. Mountain Tsunami

A secret sword art of the Chiba clan that makes use of the Orochi-Maru, a giant personal weapon that is six feet long. The user minimizes their own inertia and that of their katana while approaching an enemy at a high speed and, at the moment of impact, adds the neutralized inertia to the blade's inertia and slams the target with it. The longer the approach run, the greater the false inertial mass, reaching a maximum of ten tons.

7. Usuba Kagerou (Antlion)

A spell that uses hardening magic to anchor a five-nanometer-thick sheet of woven carbon nanotube to a perfect surface and make it a blade. The blade that Usuba Kagerou creates is sharper than any sword or razor, but the spell contains no functions to support moving the blade, demanding technical sword skill and ability from the user.

Magic Technician Development Institutes

Laboratories for the purpose of magician development that the Japanese government established one after another in response to the geopolitical climate, which had become strained prior to World War III in the 2030s. Their objectives were not to develop magic but specifically to develop magicians, researching various methods to give birth to human specimens who were most suitable for areas of magic that were considered important, including, but not limited to, genetic engineering.

Ten magic technician development institutes were established, numbered as such, and even today, five are still in operation.

The details of each institute's research are described below.

Magic Technician Development Institute One

Established in Kanazawa in 2031. Currently shut down.

Its research focus, revolving around close combat, was the development of magic that directly manipulated biological organisms. The vaporization spell Burst is derived from this facility's research. Notably, magic that could control a human body's movements was forbidden as it enabled puppet terrorism (suicide attacks using victims that had been turned into puppets).

Magic Technician Development Institute Two

Established on Awaji Island in 2031. Currently in operation. Develops magic opposite to that of Lab One, e.g. magic that can manipulate inorganic objects, especially absorption-type spells related to oxidation-reduction reactions.

Magic Technician Development Institute Three

Established in Atsugi in 2032. Currently in operation.

With its goal of developing magicians who can react to a variety of situations when operating independently, this facility is the main driver behind the research on multicasting. In particular, it tests the limits of how many spells are possible during simultaneous casting and continual casting and develops magicians who can simultaneously cast multiple spells.

Magic Technician Development Institute Four

Details unknown. Its location is speculated to be near the old prefectural border between Tokyo and Yamanashi. Its establishment is believed to have occurred in 2033. It is assumed to be shut down, but the truth of that matter is unknown. Lab Four is rumored to be the only magic research facility that was established not only with government support but also investment from private sponsors who held strong influence over the nation; it is currently operating without government oversight and being managed directly by those sponsors. Rumors also say that those sponsors actually took over control of the facility before the 2020s.

It is said their goal is to use mental interference magic to strengthen the very wellspring of the talent called magic, which exists in a magician's unconscious—the magic calculation region itself.

Magic Technician Development Institute Five

Established in Uwajima, Shikoku, in 2035. Currently in operation.

Researches magic that can manipulate various forms of matter. Its main focus, fluid control, is not technically difficult, but it has also succeeded in manipulating various solid forms. The fruits of its research include Bahamut, a spell jointly developed with the USNA. Along with the fluid-manipulation spell Abyss, it is known internationally as a magic research facility that developed two strategic-class spells.

Magic Technician Development Institute Six

Established in Sendai in 2035. Currently in operation. Researches magical heat control. Along with Lab Eight, it gives the impression of being a facility more for basic research than military purposes. However, it is said that they conducted the most genetic manipulation experiments out of all the magic technician development institutes, aside from Lab Four. (Though, of course, the full account of Lab Four's situation is not possible.)

Magic Technician Development Institute Seven

Established in Tokyo in 2036. Currently shut down.

Developed magic with an emphasis on anti-group combat. It successfully created colony control magic. Contrary to Lab Six, which was largely a nonmilitary organization, Lab Seven was established as a magician development research facility that could be relied on for assistance in defending the capital in case of an emergency.

Magic Technician Development Institute Eight

Established in Kitakyushu in 2037. Currently in operation.

Researches magical control of gravitational force, electromagnetic force, strong force, and weak force. It is a pure research institute to a greater extent than even Lab Six. However, unlike Lab Six, its relationship to the JDF is steadfast. This is because Lab Eight's research focus can be easily linked to nuclear weapons development, (though they currently avoid such connotations thanks to the JDF's seal of approval).

Magic Technician Development Institute Nine

Established in Nara in 2037. Currently shut down. This facility tried to solve several problems modern magic struggled with, such as fuzzy spell manipulation, through a fusion of modern and old magic, integrating ancient knowledge into modern techniques.

Magic Technician Development Institute Ten

Established in Tokyo in 2039. Currently shut down. Like Lab Seven, doubled as capital defense, researching area magic that could create virtual structures in space as a means of defending against high-firepower attacks. It resulted in a myriad of anti-physical barrier spells.

Lab Ten also aimed to raise magic abilities through different means from Lab Four. More specifically, rather than enhancing the magic calculation region itself, they grappled with developing magicians who responded as needed by temporarily overclocking their magic calculation regions to use powerful magic. Whether their research was successful has not been made public.

Aside from these ten institutes, other laboratories with the goal of developing Elements were operational from the 2010s to the 2020s, but they are currently all shut down. In addition, the JDF possesses a secret research facility directly under the Ground Defense Force's General Headquarters' jurisdiction, established in 2002, which is still carrying on its research. Retsu Kudou underwent enhancement operations at this institution before moving to Lab Nine.

Strategic Magicians: The Thirteen Apostles

Because modern magic was born into a highly technological world, only a few nations were able to develop strong magic for military purposes. As a result, only a handful were able to develop "strategic-class magic," which rivaled weapons of mass destruction.

However, these nations shared the magic they developed with their allies, and certain magicians of allied nations with high aptitudes for strategic-class magic came to be known as strategic magicians.

As of April 2095, there are thirteen magicians publicly recognized as strategic-class magicians by their nations. They are called the Thirteen Apostles and are considered important players in the world's military balance. The Thirteen Apostles' nations, names and strategic spell names are listed below.

USNA

Angie Sirius: Heavy Metal Burst
Elliott Miller: Leviathan
Laurent Barthes: Leviathan
* The only apostle belonging to the Stars is Angie Sirius. Elliott Miller is stationed at Alaska Base, and Laurent Barthes is stationed outside the country at Gibraltar Base. For the most part, their positions don't change.

New Soviet Union

Igor Andreivich Bezobrazov: Tuman Bomba
Leonid Kondratenko: Zemlja Armija
* As Kondratenko is of advanced age, he generally stays at the Black Sea Base.

Great Asian Alliance

Yunde Liu: Pilita (Thunderclap Tower)
*Yunde Liu died on October 31, 2095, in the battle against Japan.

Indo-Persian Federation

Barat Chandra Khan: Agni Downburst

Japan

Mio Itsuwa: Abyss

Brazil

Miguel Diez: Synchroliner Fusion
* This magic program was named by the USNA.

England

William MacLeod: Ozone Circle

Germany

Karla Schmidt: Ozone Circle
* Ozone Circle is based on a spell codeveloped by nations in the EU before its split as a means to fix the hole in the ozone layer. The magic program was perfected by England and then publicized to the old EU through a convention.

Turkey

Ali Sahin: Bahamut
* This magic program was developed in cooperation with the USNA and Japan, then provided to Turkey by Japan.

Thailand

Somchai Bunnag: Agni Downburst
* This magic program was provided by Indo-Persia.

The International Situation
State of the World in 2096

World War III, also called the Twenty Years' Global War Outbreak, was directly triggered by global cooling, and it fundamentally redrew the world map.

The USA annexed Canada and the countries from Mexico to Panama to form the United States of North America, or the USNA.

Russia reabsorbed Ukraine and Belarus to form the New Soviet Union.

China conquered northern Burma, northern Vietnam, northern Laos, and the Korean Peninsula to form the Great Asian Alliance, or GAA.

India and Iran absorbed several central Asian countries (Turkmenistan, Uzbekistan, Tajikistan, and Afghanistan) and South Asian countries (Pakistan, Nepal, Bhutan, Bangladesh, and Sri Lanka) to form the Indo-Persian Federation.

The other Asian and Arab countries formed regional military alliances to resist the three superpowers: the New Soviet Union, GAA, and the Indo-Persian Federation.

Australia chose national isolation.

The EU failed to unify and split into an eastern and a western section along the border between Germany and France. These east-west groupings also failed to properly form unions and now are actually weaker than they were before unification.

Africa saw half its nations destroyed altogether, with the surviving ones barely managing to retain urban control.

South America, excluding Brazil, fell into small, isolated states administered on a local government level.

The Irregular at
MagicHighSchool

[1]

The end of April 2097. Exact date and time not recorded. This meeting would not appear on official records.

"You can all find the details of the attack on Nansou Camp in Sergeant Major Tooyama's report."

Chief Inukai, Tsukasa Tooyama's immediate supervisor, read his subordinate's report aloud and took his seat.

"So I take it the attacker's identity has not been confirmed," a solemn attendee prompted.

"That is correct," Inukai quickly admitted. "However, given the situation, there is no doubt there *was* an attacker, and I can think of no one capable of such a role other than the Yotsuba family's own Tatsuya Shiba."

"Hmm," the attendee murmured in agreement.

"True," another chimed in.

Not a single person reproved Inukai for jumping to conclusions. In fact, all the National Defense Force Intelligence Department officials gathered had already named Tatsuya the culprit behind the attacks on Nansou Camp, the secret facility where illegal USNA operatives had been held.

The officials were correct in this case, but they would not have cared if their accusations were false. Even the Intelligence Department did not regularly draw such ruthless conclusions. Standard practice involved gathering all the evidence and testimonies they could, if only as a formality.

But this was a secret high-level meeting of the National Defense Force's Intelligence Department, an informal gathering held only when needed. Since it wasn't an official proceeding, there was no need for evidence. This was simply a forum for the officials to subjectively determine whether a particular individual or group was a viable threat to the nation.

Inukai continued: "I believe Tatsuya Shiba should be treated as dangerous and monitored more closely."

"Why not eliminate him immediately?" an attendee asked, raising a grim proposal.

"Yes, he is an ideologically dangerous person," Inukai said, "but he is also a force to be reckoned with in battle. Even without the Yotsuba family's support, his offensive abilities clearly surpass Tooyama magic. You have to admit, he is an attractive asset to have."

The chief of the Special Affairs Section took a stand. The Special Affairs Section did not officially exist within the already highly secretive Intelligence Department. Its structure was also ambiguous, sometimes consisting of one section and other times as many as thirteen.

"There is one more unconfirmed piece of information about Tatsuya Shiba that should be noted," he said.

"Oh?" The assistant director raised an eyebrow. "And what would that be, Section Chief Onda?"

The director of the Intelligence Department was not present at this meeting. Even the assistant director did not exist on public record.

"I believe everyone here is aware that Tatsuya Shiba has close ties with both the Yotsuba family and the 101st Brigade," Onda said, receiving several nods and affirmative grunts from the people at the table.

"Your point?" the assistant director asked impatiently.

"Given his position in the 101st Brigade," Onda continued, "it's possible he was the one who burned down the Jinhae Naval Port area at the end of October the year before last."

"Scorching Halloween..." A look of unease crossed the assistant director's face. Even as someone in charge of the clandestine elements of the National Defense Forces, Onda's claim didn't sit well with him.

And he was not alone. The conference room was enveloped in a heavy silence that continued unbroken until Inukai spoke up.

"Are you saying that mysterious strategic magician is actually Tatsuya Shiba?"

Inukai, too, was someone who kept to the shadows due to his routine involvement in unlawful activities. He understood the significant position strategic magicians occupied within the National Defense Force. If Tatsuya was in fact the magician who had been responsible for the Scorching Halloween, it would not be easy to dispose of him.

"This is still unconfirmed," Onda responded. "But even if it turns out to be true, we cannot simply ignore him and his dangerous tendencies."

He was the only person in the room without a look of astonishment plastered on his face.

"In fact," he continued, "I believe it would be wrong to turn a blind eye to any individual with so much power."

Onda asserted his opinion in a manner typical of someone who was part of an extrajudicial organization: deliberately devoid of military terminology. Reassured by this unwavering stance, the assistant director regained his composure.

"You're absolutely right," he nodded. "We will deal with Tatsuya in accordance with our reeducation policies."

"Agreed."

"That would be for the best."

The meeting attendees voiced their agreement with the assistant director one after another.

At the end of April, Lieutenant Colonel Kazama and his detachment returned to the 101st Brigade after their dispatch to Hokkaido.

"I and the other 195 personnel have just returned," Kazama reported.

The Independent Magic Battalion he commanded was a battalion in name only. In reality, their troop strength was only two companies' worth. Kazama's latest deployment had involved half that, totaling 195 soldiers. His report confirmed there had been no casualties under his watch.

"It's good to have you all back," the brigade commander, Major General Saeki, replied with an expression of relief.

She knew losses were an inevitable in combat, but there was nothing better than hearing there had been zero casualties. This was particularly true for the Independent Magic Battalion, which was an experimental unit for magic weapons and tactics and incorporated several magicians with special abilities. Morality aside, the value of these magicians as military personnel was decidedly higher than that of other units.

While Saeki had been kept apprised of Kazama's situation from daily reports, it was an immense relief to personally confirm everyone had returned safely.

"Lieutenant Colonel," she said, "I'm granting you and your unit three days' special leave. During that time, you are all free to go off-base if you wish."

"Thank you, ma'am. My soldiers will be happy to hear that." Kazama's lips relaxed into a slight smile as he stood at ease.

Saeki nodded. Then she closed her eyes and let out a small sigh. When she opened her eyes again, her expression hardened into one fitting of the National Defense Force's most prominent general. Kazama tensed.

"I received news from Major Onda yesterday," Saeki said.

"Major Onda?" Kazama puzzled. "I don't think I know him."

As was customary for a member of the military, Kazama read through all the personnel news without fail. He couldn't claim to have memorized everything he'd read, but he was confident in his knowledge about all officers ranked colonel and above. That said, he had no recollection of a Major Onda.

"He is the section chief of Special Affairs," Saeki explained.

"You mean for the Intelligence Department," Kazama clarified.

Saeki had no direct authority over the Intelligence Department. Therefore, an Intelligence section chief was not obligated to report to her. That could only mean the connection between the two was personal. Major Onda must have been one of Major General Saeki's sources of information, and vice versa. At least, that was how Kazama understood it.

He continued: "So what did he tell you?"

"Apparently, Specialist Ooguro has made it onto the Intelligence Department's purge list," Saeki immediately replied. "For attacking their secret camp."

"They're trying to eliminate him?" Kazama asked, his voice stable but bewildered.

"Execution isn't on the table, if that's what you're asking," Saeki replied. "They are simply planning to capture and reeducate him."

"That's ridiculous," Kazama muttered.

The way he said this made it sound as if he was doubting Saeki, rather than the Intelligence Department.

"I agree," Saeki said carefully. "After all, reeducation—well, there's no need to mince words here. *Brainwashing* tends to significantly impair magic abilities."

"That's not what I meant, ma'am," Kazama insisted.

Uncertain what Kazama was getting at, Saeki implicitly urged him on.

"What I was trying to say," the lieutenant colonel continued, "is that assassinating the specialist may be possible. Attempting to capture him, on the other hand, is a hopeless waste of effort. The Intelligence Department's demise would be the least of our worries. Worst-case scenario, Tokyo might drown in a sea of flames."

Saeki gave Kazama a stern look, almost as if she suspected Kazama himself to be scheming such imminent destruction.

"Do you really think the specialist would go that far?" she asked.

"All I will say is that naming him as a potential threat was the correct move," Kazama replied. "The specialist is the most narcissistic person I have ever met. He would never sacrifice himself or those close to him for the sake of his nation. Men like him aren't cut out for military work."

"Yes, he may have incomparable abilities, but personality-wise, he is just as you say." Saeki clearly agreed Tatsuya lacked what it took to be a true public servant.

"However," Kazama added, "Intelligence underestimates how dangerous he can be. Even without using Material Burst, the specialist could destroy a whole city in a single night."

"You seem to think pretty highly of him," Saeki noted.

"If reality were a game, I'd say he is strong enough to be the final boss," Kazama said.

"But if he's the final boss, where is the hero who will lead us to a happy ending?"

"Well, they haven't shown up yet, if they even exist. In a perfect world, we'd keep our final boss busy until that hero appears."

Both Kazama and Saeki let out a simultaneous sigh and scoffed. They suddenly felt ridiculous for seriously considering fantastical things like final bosses and heroes.

Then Saeki spoke: "I will convey your concerns to the Intelligence Department through Major Onda. Although I'm not sure how much of a difference it will make. Thank you for your hard work, colonel. You are free to go."

"Ma'am."

Kazama saluted the major general and left her office.

◇ ◇ ◇

It was after school on May 2. Unaware that people were treating him like a final boss, Tatsuya returned to his daily routine. And he wasn't the only one.

The incident at the end of April involving Shiina's kidnapping had been wrapped up as a misunderstanding caused by a lack of communication. By now, First High had practically forgotten it had even happened. Miyuki and Minami had also experienced the attack on the finishing school around the same time. Luckily, the girls' nonchalant expressions didn't give other students any reason to suspect anything out of the ordinary.

And so, after-school days returned to normal. On this day, Tatsuya and the other members of the student council went about their duties as usual.

Since the day before, they had been preparing for the Nine School Competition in addition to their regular office work. The guidelines for this year's event had not yet arrived, but they had started off with some basic preparations that wouldn't be affected by event changes, like the ones of the previous year.

Tatsuya was busy checking the competition CAD catalog. The competition placed restrictions on the specifications of CADs. Specifically, their hardware performance had to be kept within certain limits. But the lack of limits on software meant practically speaking, the storage-access speed and OS's usability were the biggest factors, assuming hardware was comparable.

Just as events could be changed, the regulations for CADs could be changed as well. But gathering information on CADs was by no means a waste of time. Tatsuya, who was involved in CAD production as Taurus Silver, was not completely knowledgeable about the outdated models. While claiming this research was part of his student council duties, he found it enjoyable. Just as he was getting into his work, a voice called out to him.

"Master," Pixie said aloud, rather than telepathically.

"What is it?" Tatsuya answered without taking his eyes away from his screen.

"I have received. Important. News," she replied.

He spun around. "What news?"

"It is. Related to. Strategic magic."

Tatsuya made eye contact with Miyuki before replying, "Screen it on the wall."

Pixie obediently rewound the news program she was in the process of recording and displayed it on the wall. All the student council members turned their heads to watch. It was just out of curiosity at first, but their gazes became increasingly intense as the program progressed. Someone even gasped sharply halfway through. But no one dared to say a word until it was over.

"First South America and now Africa?" Izumi was the first to break the silence.

Honoka spoke next: "The Gulf of Guinea and the Niger Delta region... Weren't those areas practically controlled by the Great Asian Alliance?"

"Yeah," Shizuku answered vaguely.

"Well, it *is* a war zone," Tatsuya said. "More likely that strategic magic is used there than Europe or North America. But still..."

He couldn't hide his own surprise. The news program had just reported that the strategic magic spell, Thunderclap Tower, had been cast in the Niger Delta region, resulting in many casualties. This had been followed by a statement from the Great Asian Alliance's army acknowledging the event.

As Tatsuya had feared, the Synchroliner Fusion incident in South America had lowered the psychological hurdle of using strategic magic. For those who used it, that is.

But it had also made society—and the world as a whole—more critical of its use. The voices condemning the Brazilian army's decision to cast Synchroliner Fusion had surged in from all over the world. Even a month after the incident, things had not blown over.

Despite this, the Great Asian Alliance did not bother to hide its use of strategic magic. They even went as far as to publicly announce the use of Thunderclap Tower, as if they were proud to show off the results of their battle.

"Is this their way of keeping France in check?" Miyuki asked.

"That's probably their main objective, yes," Tatsuya replied.

During the Twenty Years' Global War Outbreak, Africa had been flooded with great powers in search of resources. Fighting had broken out among various factions—nation against nation, and government forces against rebel groups. The great powers had primarily been interested in securing the resource-rich territories, and to obtain access to them, they had sent various forms of aid, intervened from the shadows, or directly engaged with the warring forces. Ultimately, these actions had led to the disappearance of entire nations on the African continent.

This conflict had persisted for more than thirty years after the formal end of the war, albeit on a smaller and more sporadic scale. In the Gulf of Guinea region, the Great Asian Alliance and France had been engaged in a fragmented, chess-like struggle, vying for control of territory that was mostly occupied by a patchwork of small, armed tribes.

In the Niger Delta region, the Great Asian Alliance had maintained control over a consolidated territory for several years. However, in recent months, armed groups had begun claiming to be descendants of an organization active in the early twenty-first century called MEND (Movement for the Emancipation of the Niger Delta). These groups, supported by France, threatened the Great Asian Alliance's dominance.

It was fair to assume the strategic magic spell reported on the news had been aimed at checking and curtailing French support.

"Could there be any other objectives?"

This time, it was Izumi who posed a question. She still hadn't warmed up to Tatsuya yet. In fact, it was rare for her to talk directly to him like this. But her curiosity had gotten the better of her on this day.

"The strategic magic spell the Great Asian Alliance claim to have cast was Thunderclap Tower," Tatsuya replied in a roundabout way. "But they said the caster was a girl called Lirei Liu, not Yunde Liu."

"Maybe this was their way of announcing a new strategic class magician," Izumi offered.

"There's no doubt about that," Tatsuya agreed. "But it also means they've lost their ability to hide."

"Hide what?" Izumi puzzled. Honoka and Shiina also looked confused.

Tatsuya explained. "Yunde Liu disappeared from the public eye over a year ago. He was even absent from the military parade he attended every year. There have been rumors among military personnel about his possible death. At this point, the Great Asian Alliance can't hide the truth anymore."

He knew Yunde Liu had lost his life in battle during the Scorching Halloween incident, but the Great Asian Alliance had kept this information a secret. He spoke to the student council members in a way that suggested he was at least somewhat in the know.

"So you're telling us Yunde Liu is dead and Lirei Liu is his successor?" Izumi clarified.

"Right." Tatsuya nodded. "Publicizing the existence of a strategic magician serves as a deterrent. The only reason for the Great Asian Alliance to announce Lirei Liu is to reveal Yunde Liu may be dead, but there is another strategic magician ready to replace him."

"Oh, I get it now," Izumi murmured. "This whole thing is both a warning for France and a demonstration to the world."

A few hours later, Tatsuya and Miyuki met up with Leo, Erika, and some other seniors at Café Einebrise. There, too, the main topic of conversation was the strategic magic spell cast in Africa. As the conversation continued, Tatsuya ended up once again explaining why the Great Asian Alliance had publicly admitted to their use of strategic magic.

"But wouldn't that provoke neighboring countries?" Erika commented.

"I'm sure they were well aware of that possibility. Deterrence, after all, is essentially a threat."

This sounded like something Tatsuya would say, but it was Mikihiko who had said it. Though out of character for a good-natured guy like him, his perspective was common for boys his age.

"What I'm more surprised about," Leo chimed in, "is that this new Thirteen Apostles member is only fourteen. That's even younger than us."

Within an hour of the initial news report, a justification for the legitimacy of the strategic magic spell had been made, which had included a promotional speech about the new Apostle.

Recent news had only publicized the strategic magician's name, Lirei Liu, and her gender. Mikihiko wasn't the only one who had been surprised when the Great Asian Alliance had announced her age.

"I'm more shocked about how tiny the girl is," Honoka chimed in with a worried look.

"You can say that again," Mizuki agreed with a similar expression. "I know the situation is different for every country, but it doesn't seem like she'll survive."

"Sure, I feel bad the kid has been forced to be a puppet, but she *did* just get officially recognized by her country. That's not the worst situation to be in," Erika said with a tinge of spite in her voice. She knew both Japan and the Great Asian Alliance had a history of sacrificing children Lirei's age in magic experiments. In fact, this tragic pattern was a global phenomenon. Since many victims were buried in the darkness, in a certain sense, Erika considered Lirei lucky to be pushed into the limelight.

"I was surprised they publicized the girl's face," Shizuku said, speaking up before Erika's statement could put a damper on everyone's mood.

"Yes, it is rare," Miyuki agreed. "Most countries do everything they can to hide all information about their strategic magicians, including their faces."

While her goal was to help move the conversation into a more positive light, her shock at seeing Lirei's face on international news had been genuine.

"It's only surprising if that girl is really the one who cast Thunderclap Tower," Tatsuya cautioned.

Everyone at the table was taken aback. They'd forgotten to consider the possibility that Lirei Liu was nothing more than a face for the cameras.

"Although," Tatsuya continued, "I doubt the Great Asian Alliance's military would make a girl like that a symbol for morale."

"Unless they wanted to say something like, 'Look at this girl trying her best. You adults better step it up'?" Erika teased.

This silly interpretation of Tatsuya's speculation made her earlier flash of anger seem like a fluke.

"Sure," Tatsuya said with a deliberately wry smile. He understood how Erika felt.

"Wasn't the Great Asian Alliance's recognition of Yunde Liu's death in battle also to reinforce the image of a faithful child who follows in her grandfather's footsteps?" Mikihiko prompted.

"That is, if she really *is* his granddaughter," Erika interjected with a devious smile.

The Great Asian Alliance had presented Lirei Liu as Yunde's granddaughter. Whether this was true or not was still up for debate.

"On a different note..." Leo began, but he paused.

Mikihiko glanced over at his friend. "What's up?"

Leo hesitated before blurting out his question. "Is it true eight hundred people were killed? Maybe they weren't lying about there being very few civilians living in the war-torn area. But isn't eight hundred too few? I mean, we're dealing with strategic magic here, right?"

GREAT ASIAN ALLIANCE:
NNOUNCEMENT OF STRATEGIC MAGICIAN

Everyone turned to Tatsuya.

"Well, it makes sense this strategic magic results in fewer casualties than Synchroliner Fusion," Tatsuya replied. "Thunderclap Tower is a spell designed more to destroy factories and infrastructures than to directly harm or kill people."

"So it's not a spell that hits people with lightning?" Mizuki asked with a look of total confusion.

"Thunderclap Tower consists of two types of magic," Tatsuya explained. "One triggers a sort of electric avalanche over a target area, and the other lowers electric resistance throughout the same area in a sporadic and uneven way."

Mizuki still looked completely mystified. Tatsuya turned to Mikihiko, who was always trying to show Mizuki his good side.

Mikihiko took a stab at clarifying the situation. "In simple terms, the magic that triggers an electric avalanche creates the electric charge needed for the lightning. Lowering an area's electric resistance in an uneven way essentially breaks down the effects of insulation. Repeatedly lowering the resistance at short intervals helps generate a continuous series of lightning strikes."

"In other words," Mizuki said slowly, "Thunderclap Tower is a spell that continuously rains down lots of lightning?"

She had been staring intently at Mikihiko throughout his explanation, determined not to miss a single word. Yet it seemed she was still having difficulty understanding.

"Yeah, that sounds about right," Mikihiko responded generously. Whether he would be so charitable for anyone other than Mizuki was impossible to tell.

"What's most important to understand here," he continued, "is that Thunderclap Tower is characterized by its emphasis on the number of strikes rather than the power of a single shot."

He glanced over at Tatsuya, who gave him a silent nod. Perhaps he had been unsure of his own explanation, because this reassuring gesture allowed to Mikihiko breathe a sigh of relief.

More confident now, he went on. "So instead of a superpowerful lightning bolt hitting one target, it rains down reasonably strong lightning bolts over a wide area. It's the kind of spell that would be a nightmare for lightly equipped infantry, but as long as the target takes some precautions against lightning, there's a decent chance of surviving. The only problem is it has an unexpected side effect."

"The destruction of infrastructure?" Mizuki ventured.

"Right," Mikihiko nodded. "Intermittent lightning strikes during short intervals means the electromagnetic field in the target area fluctuates continuously and rapidly. Moreover, the spell drops the electric resistance of all objects in the area to a level that just barely causes an electrical breakdown. Without going into too much detail, this means Thunderclap Tower can cause serious damage to electronic equipment over a massive area."

"In other words, it's a magic EMP weapon," Leo interjected.

"The underlying principles are different, but based purely on the effects, I guess you could say that," Mikihiko replied. He surprisingly wasn't upset at his friend for interrupting his conversation with Mizuki.

"Okay," Leo mused. "The spell doesn't have super-high killing power, so there were fewer deaths. I think I can understand that. But that brings up another question."

"And what's that?" Mikihiko asked.

"The spell's target area is a war zone where fighting has been going on for a long time. Wouldn't that mean the only damaged machinery would have been resource-extraction equipment?"

"I'm not exactly sure, but you're probably right."

"But the Great Asian Alliance controls most of the mining facilities in that area right now," Leo contended. "If that's the case, wouldn't they just be damaging their own equipment? Why would they use a spell that just hurts themselves?"

Mikihiko glanced at Tatsuya for help.

Tatsuya began speaking slowly without panic or fuss. "Rumor

has it the Great Asian Alliance's power in the Niger Delta region has recently fallen. Because of the unmanned automatic weapons provided by France, about half the area they previously controlled has been seized by hostile armed groups."

Something in Tatsuya's explanation seemed to ring a bell.

"Unmanned automatic weapons... Right..." Leo murmured.

"That makes sense," Mikihiko nodded, having reached the same understanding. "The Great Asian Alliance prioritized neutralizing the unmanned automatic weapons, even if it meant damaging their mining facilities."

Despite the proud looks on the two boys' faces, Tatsuya didn't give them full marks. Instead, he said, "The motivation for using Thunderclap Tower in their own territory was likely to counter the unmanned weapons. However, it goes without saying the spell still has the power to kill. It can easily take the lives of lightly equipped soldiers without adequate protection or civilians in plain clothes."

Leo and Mikihiko went stiff. They had forgotten the number of human casualties had not been zero.

"Are you saying the actual number of casualties is much higher than what was reported?" Mikihiko asked cautiously.

"The problem with Thunderclap Tower is, it can even paralyze medical facilities," Tatsuya answered with a clouded expression. "Even if they don't die instantly, there will be quite a lot of casualties."

[2]

Two years ago, at the 295th Nine School Competition, Tatsuya had had Shizuku use a spell he had invented called Active Air Mine. As a result, Shizuku had been crowned the Speed Shooting champion in the rookie competition, and Active Air Mine had been recorded as a new spell in the Magic University's Encyclopedia of Magic.

However, at the time, the Yotsuba family had always treated Tatsuya as a pariah or simply a problematic member of the family, so he hadn't liked being in the limelight. Instead of telling people he had invented the spell, he'd tried to register Shizuku as its developer. But Shizuku wasn't one to take credit for someone else's work. Ultimately, Active Air Mine had only been provisionally recorded with its developer marked as unknown.

In fact, the spell hadn't been officially recorded until the January of this year. Once the Yotsuba family had named Tatsuya "son of the head of the family" and "fiancé of the clan heiress," there had no longer been any need to hide the fact that he had developed the spell. Yet Tatsuya hadn't come forward. The National Magic University had long known Tatsuya was the true developer and had been approaching him regularly since the Nine School Competition. They had finally realized there must have been some deeper reason for his hesitation to reveal himself once his new status had been announced to the public. Soon after the new year had begun, they'd called yet again to persuade him to take credit for the spell. It was only then that Tatsuya had agreed with the constant insistence that it would only look bad to have this spell be provisional forever.

While he hadn't initially been keen on the idea, Tatsuya was glad he had registered himself as the Active Air Mine developer now. After the morning news, he was sincerely grateful not to have to bother Shizuku with the spell.

Tatsuya's seat was by the aisle window, just like the year prior. Before school began, there were a noticeable number of students looking in his direction and whispering in the Class 3-E classroom.

Mikihiko leaned on Tatsuya's desk. "Is it true what they say about armed guerrilla forces using Active Air Mine? It did have tactical destructive power, but I didn't think it was that formidable."

He had come all the way from his own classroom to Class E, not out of curiosity but out of concern for Tatsuya.

"Active Air Mine has no upper limit to its power," Tatsuya replied nonchalantly. "While there is a trade-off in size and speed, the power can be increased as much as the caster wants. I appreciate your concern, but judging by the condition of the victims, I'm almost positive they used my spell."

Mikihiko's expression clouded over as the whispers in the classroom gained momentum. Needless to say, the topic on the students' lips was the news appearing on every media platform that morning.

Two days ago, the strategic magic spell cast in Africa had left several dead or in critical condition. The Great Asian Alliance, which effectively controlled the area, had reported the death toll as less than nine hundred as of the day before. Based on the spell's scale, however, it was safe to say there was a much larger number of casualties. The Western media even estimated the actual number of deaths among locals alone to be over three thousand.

This number probably included armed guerrillas. There were

probably even a few terrorists mixed in. But it was certain that civilians were also among the dead.

The night before, a reprisal had taken place—a group of armed guerrillas had attacked a Great Asian Alliance military base in Central Asia. The organization responsible for the attack was the Emancipation Army of the Niger Delta (EAND), an armed group that called themselves successors to an international terrorist organization known as the Movement for the Emancipation of the Niger Delta (MEND).

Timing-wise, EAND had been planning to attack the military base before the strategic spell Thunderclap Tower had been cast. The claim that they had been retaliating in response to the indiscriminate electric attacks was only an afterthought. Nevertheless, this did not change the fact that the surprise attack had been carried out as an act of vengeance.

Efea Mensah, a magician from the Gulf of Guinea's west coast and central figure of the attack, was the spokeswoman for the successful attack. The spell she had used in the base was Active Air Mine. This was a spell that made solid objects vulnerable and crushed them with an oscillating field that generated sparse but dense waves. It had only been recently discovered that a person caught in the field would have all the bones in their body crushed, such turning the victim into a sack of blood. Efea Mensah was the first magician to have used the spell on another human being.

Erika spoke up. "Tatsuya. Just because a spell you created killed people, doesn't mean it was your fault. The magician who pulled the trigger is to blame."

She irritably clicked her tongue. Most of Tatsuya's classmates awkwardly turned away from him, with one exception—Chiaki Hirakawa.

"I don't know about that," she muttered loud enough for Tatsuya to hear. "Developing inhumane magic carries a moral responsibility."

"What'd you say?!" Erika shouted, her eyes flashing dangerously. But Chiaki simply turned her cheek.

"Stop it, Erika," Tatsuya said.

Meanwhile, a group of girls huddled around Chiaki.

"Moral responsibility, you say?" Leo muttered with a disinterested tone. "What about Nobel's dynamite? Einstein's atomic bomb? People just love naming a scapegoat. And I'm afraid there's only going to be more where that came from."

Unfortunately, no one present could deny his prediction.

"Do you mean to say the Magic University refuses to take responsibility for this incident?"

"The Magic University serves only as a research institution in charge of compiling research results within the Encyclopedia of Magic."

An overbearing reporter was interviewing a Magic University representative in charge of making reports on public television. The representative's voice was firm, but his complexion was pale, possibly a sign he was intimidated by the reporter's intensity.

"Then is the First High student who developed the spell responsible for this lethal magic?" the reporter asked.

The malice that filled this question made the representative's face completely change color.

"The First High student is not to blame at all!" he countered.

But even this enraged retort didn't slow the reporter down at all.

"However," the reporter pressed, "you can't deny that more than a hundred people have died as a result of the spell this First High student developed for the National Magic High School Goodwill Competition Magic Tournament."

"All of those victims died in *battle*," the representative corrected. "The responsibility for that should only be borne by the guerrillas who used the spell as a weapon, not by the person who created it."

"Are you sure about that?" the reporter prompted.

"What do you mean?" the representative asked.

The reporter grinned slyly, as if he had been waiting precisely for this question.

"Well," he began, "conventional weapons and needlessly cruel weapons, such as poison gas and expanding bullets, are regulated by the international treaty. Inhumane weapons are designated as illegal."

"Active Air Mine is not a weapon!" The university representative's face turned even redder than before as he began to understand what the reporter was implying. Unfortunately, his increasingly sharp tone couldn't stop the reporter from running his mouth.

"But, sir, it was clearly used as a weapon."

"Wh-while that may be true," the representative stammered, "it is only the caster who should be blamed."

The reporter switched tack and subtly moved the goalposts. "Don't you think since the spell has *mine* in its name, there was some intention to use it as a weapon from the very beginning?"

The university representative was at a loss for how to refute the reporter's assumptions. Modern magic was largely developed for use in combat. Especially since most of the magic included in the Magic University's Encyclopedia of Magic could be used for military purposes, it was difficult to argue Active Air Mine was an exception.

The reporter continued: "The consensus of international organizations is that inhumane weapons are illegal to possess or develop. To prevent our country from being singled out as an enemy of humanity on the global stage, shouldn't universities provide appropriate guidance to their students and the students at their affiliated high schools?"

"In the case of this spell developed by a Japanese individual that was used in armed conflict in Central Asia, our university believes the responsibility lies solely with the party who used it," the university representative concluded.

Ultimately, this was the only logic he could muster to push through the rest of the press conference.

* * *

The press conference at the Magic University was being held on a Sunday. Though this day of the week was unusual, it indicated how urgent the university perceived the situation as.

Once the screening of the live event was over, Miyuki immediately asked Tatsuya, "Is it true the international community has banned the possession and development of inhumane weapons?"

The two had been watching the conference together on their living room television. It had been four months since they had officially stopped being siblings, but Miyuki's habit of treating Tatsuya like her older brother wasn't quick to change. Lately, she had even justified her behavior with statements like, "It's not a problem as long as no one else is around."

Tatsuya decided to let it slide for the sake of answering her question.

"I'm not sure," he said. "*Possession* of inhumane weapons is definitely illegal, but it would be a challenge to ban the development of new weapons altogether. Whether a weapon is inhumane or not isn't always clear until its actual creation."

"You mean a weapon's potential danger can't be known until it is used?" Miyuki clarified.

"Actually, it's fairly clear by the design phase what a weapon will be. After all, each weapon is made with a purpose," Tatsuya responded with a smile. "The tricky part is that it's more common to keep new weapons secret until they're finished. A developer who discloses his plan before completion is usually confident the weapon won't be classified as inhumane."

"Oh, that's what you meant."

"Magic, on the other hand, is a completely different story," Tatsuya explained. "For example, airplanes weren't developed as weapons, but they have been adapted for military use. The way magic is used depends on the skill and intent of the magician using it. Something not originally designed for military use sometimes has the potential to become a weapon for assassination or even mass destruction."

A quiet sigh escaped his lips before he continued.

"To be honest, I didn't think there was a magician out there who could use Active Air Mine to this extent. Talk about a close call. I'm just relieved we managed to avoid causing any trouble for Shizuku."

There was a sense of resignation in Tatsuya's words, but Miyuki couldn't tell where it was coming from. This made it all the more difficult for her to find the right words to say.

From a logical standpoint, Tatsuya bore no responsibility for the casualties among the Great Asian Alliance's military personnel and base workers as a result of Active Air Mine. Unfortunately, things didn't work out so neatly in the real world. At least not in the short term.

Tatsuya understood this, of course. But he had not anticipated that the repercussions would manifest as they did on the Friday afternoon of May 10, 2097.

Immediately after Miyuki returned to the student council office after having been called to the main office, she stood near the entrance facing away from her seat and addressed the room.

"Everyone, please listen closely," she said in a tone anyone could tell hinted something wasn't right.

Tatsuya, Honoka, Izumi, Minami, and Shiina fixed their gazes on the student council president as she looked on the verge of tears.

"I just received word from the Nine School Competition Committee that…this year's Nine School Competition has been canceled," Miyuki announced.

Her voice quivered slightly, but she was surprisingly composed given the news. Meanwhile, Honoka and Izumi were agape, and Minami and Shiina were frozen in shock. It even took Tatsuya a few seconds to put his thoughts into words.

"…Miyuki, can I see the correspondence letter?" he finally managed.

"Of course," she responded. "Just a moment."

Miyuki awkwardly walked over to her seat and turned to her terminal.

"Here it is," she said.

Tatsuya waited until her fingers stopped flying across the screen to check the student council shared drive and open the newly added file. The other four student council members, who had been in a trance, followed Tatsuya's lead and opened the file on their own terminals.

"I knew it," Tatsuya muttered after reading through the letter. "This is all my fault."

"It's not!" Miyuki yelled, the feelings she had been suppressing boiling over into anger. "This is slander! You aren't to blame at all!"

The office's temperature suddenly dropped. Not only had Miyuki let her emotions get the better of her, but she'd lost control of her magic as well.

"Miyuki, calm down."

Understanding her anger was for his sake, Tatsuya's voice lacked its usual intensity. Instead of scolding her, he extended his left index and middle fingers, waving them slightly right to left. Suddenly, the office's temperature returned to normal. The frost that had clung to the windows disappeared completely, and there was not even condensation left in its wake.

"You turned back time…?" Shiina gasped.

She wasn't the only one surprised. All five girls, including Miyuki, had heard a phantom sound, as if a magnetic tape had been rewound. This was a side effect of Tatsuya's Regenerate spell, which had helped him counter the freezing magic Miyuki had unleashed. The spell worked by reverting the information associated with the room's progressing cooling process to its state before Miyuki's magic had been cast. The world had then reconciled the event that had occurred by having the cooling phenomenon reverse itself. The phantom sounds Shiina and the others had heard were noise from the psionic waves generated when the reversal of cause and effect in the information body dimension had clashed with the normal flow of causality.

"Forgive me, Tatsuya," Miyuki apologized, realizing her reckless use of magic had caused trouble for him. This realization helped cool her head, and she regained her composure.

"But I truly believe you're not to blame," she continued. "The cancellation of the Nine School Competition is a result of the irresponsible actions of the competition committee. In fact, the competition has been receiving a lot of criticism lately based on their event changes last year."

"Th-that's right!" Honoka chimed in. "The whole Active Air Mine fiasco just started the other day! Last year's competition and its strong military focus is the real problem."

Just as Miyuki and Honoka had explained, doing their best to comfort Tatsuya, the media had been hysterically demanding that someone take responsibility for the development of inhumane magic until the Monday after the Magic University's press conference. As soon as Tuesday had rolled around, though, the focus had suddenly shifted to the nature of the Nine School Competition itself. The decision to include the Cross-Country Steeplechase event in particular had been condemned as a sign of military involvement in the Magic University's affiliated high schools.

There was some basis for this criticism. Cross-Country Steeplechase was essentially military exercises turned into a competitive sport. It had even been created with the intention of allowing military personnel to compete and showcase the results of their training.

This event wasn't the only one of its kind. Shields Down was an adaptation of Close Quarters Combat (CQC) training. Many students reckoned even Rower and Gunner was an event derived from navy training programs.

It was hard to say if there was any manipulation involved in the whole ordeal. Shizuku's father may have taken action to protect his daughter from becoming a victim of the media. Military corporations involved in producing conventional weapons may have even tried to halt the military's use of magic to prevent a decline in their business from magic replacing weapons.

If the latter was true, it might be possible to say their scheme was successful. Having unexpectedly been under fire, the competition committee had expressed regret that a Magic High School student's wholesome invention had been exploited by armed forces. They had then used this as a pretext to cancel this year's competition, citing the need to review the security on their information management system.

"You're right," Tatsuya said. "I'm sorry for making you worry."

He accepted Miyuki and Honoka's reassurances and offered an apology for his self-deprecating remarks. At least on the surface.

Unfortunately, not all Magic High School students believed the Nine School Competition's cancellation was solely due to a lax management system that needed to be reviewed. In fact, very few students took the committee's excuses at face value.

"Shippou, did you hear?"

Senkawa, a club member in the same grade as Takuma, approached him during club. The two boys had been teammates in the previous year's Monolith Code event.

"If you're talking about the Nine School Competition, I just heard the news," Takuma replied, trying his best to remain calm. But despite his efforts, his tone revealed a sense of disappointment.

"We both still have hopes for next year, but this must really be tough on the seniors. They were probably looking forward to a successful final year," Senkawa said with sympathy.

"Uh-huh," Takuma replied apathetically.

Regrettably, Senkawa didn't realize this was a hint for him to drop the subject and continued, "It's only going to be canceled this year, right?"

"The committee said they just needed to review their information management system security, so probably."

"Good," Senkawa said earnestly with a sigh. "I hope that's true.

But you know all this talk about information management is just an excuse, right? Unless the committee does something drastic like eliminating combat-style competitions or restricting the use of magic, won't it be hard to hold the competition next year?"

Takuma frowned. Assuming his comment was to blame, Senkawa quickly reasoned, "I mean, it's not every day a high schooler's spell gets used in warfare. I doubt Shiba saw this coming."

"It's not Shiba's fault the Nine School Competition got canceled." Takuma scowled and spoke in a tone angrier than he intended.

Senkawa hadn't expected this reaction. He quickly justified himself.

"Th-the thought never crossed my mind! Shiba is clearly a victim of the media's antics. But…" He trailed off with a glance at Takuma's expression.

"But what?"

Senkawa took this as a signal to continue. "Don't you think Shiba could have predicted his spell would be used for military purposes? And even used to kill?"

Takuma's expression twisted into a frown again. Not because he found Senkawa's statement unsettling, but because he remembered the images of the victims the Great Asian Alliance had released. They were horrifically graphic. An age restriction had immediately been applied to them, but unfortunately, Takuma had stumbled upon them on a self-proclaimed freelance journalist's news site.

"It's not like Shiba had to create a spell like that," Senkawa said. "Kitayama could have won the Speed Shooting event on her own. Doesn't that make you think Shiba might have been reckless and taken things too far? I dunno…"

Takuma's lack of responsiveness made Senkawa trail off again. But Takuma's silence wasn't because he disagreed. In fact, he felt deep down that his friend had a point.

First High had its fair share of students who were on Tatsuya's side. They hadn't forgotten about his contributions to their victory in the Nine School Competition in years past. Even those who had reservations about supporting him were hesitant to criticize him openly. Students from other schools, on the other hand, were a completely different story.

Masaki Ichijou was seated in Third High's Disciplinary Committee office. Even though he wasn't the committee president, he held a prominent position in the committee that was widely acknowledged by every student, including the committee president himself. In fact, Masaki was the de facto Third High student leader. Even the student council president recognized him as such. Third High's student council president wasn't from one of the twenty-eight families. She wasn't even from one of the Hundred Families. Even so, Masaki was the only student at Third High who stood in a position higher than her.

In any case, Masaki was in the Disciplinary Committee office waiting for some work to come up. Unlike at First High, Third High's Disciplinary Committee operated in response to student reports rather than emphasizing regular patrols. Just then, one of Masaki's classmate and one of his juniors came running in.

"Masaki!" "Ichijou!" the boys called out simultaneously.

"What is it?" he asked.

All three boys had been teammates during the previous Nine School Competition. Masaki's junior had been this year's upcoming ace.

"Is it true the Nine School Competition has been canceled?" the junior asked.

Masaki sighed. "Yes, it's true. I just heard the news myself."

"Is it that guy from First High's fault?" the classmate chimed in.

He was clearly talking about Tatsuya. Both the previous year and the year before that, Third High's defeats at Tatsuya's hands had made him an official Third High enemy.

"No," Masaki said firmly. "The committee is just reviewing its information management security so no other spells created at the Nine School Competition make their way into the hands of guerrillas and terrorists."

He wasn't the biggest fan of Tatsuya, either. The two boys had been on the same side during the Gu Jie incident, but Masaki still considered Tatsuya his rival. In fact, because they were rivals, it didn't feel right to speak badly of him. Tatsuya would always be the bad guy in Masaki's mind, but he felt he should confront Tatsuya openly and fairly. Making false accusations would be a cowardly move. His classmate and junior, on the other hand, didn't share the same sentiment. It was easy for them to focus their anger and frustration on Tatsuya.

"But it was that guy's inhumane magic that sparked the review in the first place," Masaki's classmate said.

"That's right," the junior chimed in. "Formalities aside, he's the main cause."

"Well, his magic was the trigger, but…" Masaki trailed off.

Despite his respect for Tatsuya, it was also true these guys were on his team and Tatsuya was their enemy. Defending Tatsuya in front of his teammates wasn't the easiest thing to do.

"I knew it," the junior said. "I'm so angry, Ichijou. Why aren't we allowed to compete in the Nine School Competition because of something he did?"

"That's what I want to know," the classmate agreed. "Couldn't we just have the competition without First High? Or just without him?"

"That's impossible," Masaki shook his head. "Unless you want the media accusing the competition of discrimination on top of everything else."

Even to Masaki, arguing Tatsuya should be kicked out of the competition seemed a little too extreme. He tried to reel his former teammates in.

"Well, I guess you're right," his classmate said. "As long as he's involved, we'll never catch a break."

"Everyone calling him a genius engineer for so long must have gone to his head," his junior added. "Now he thinks he can get away with anything."

Unfortunately, Masaki's efforts hadn't found receptive ears.

Similar conversations unfolded at the other magic high schools. But none of these schools staged protests directed at First High. The official statements from every branch was that there was no direct connection between the Nine School Competition's cancellation and the military use of Active Air Mine. Unfortunately, once Saturday rolled around and more details of the cancellation became public, personal attacks against Tatsuya did occur. It was at this difficult time that news from America arrived, driving Tatsuya into a corner.

[3]

The news reported first thing in the morning on Sunday, May 12 was about an international project announced at 1 PM local time in Los Angeles the day before.

The presenter of the project was a man named Edward Clark. Clark was a government-employed engineer working for the National Science Agency (NSA), and his statement was a call for cooperation from the NSA to the countries of the world.

The project he spoke about was called the Dione Project—an international effort launched unilaterally by the USNA without any completed groundwork to date. In other words, it was a dream project; it aimed to terraform Venus with resources from Jupiter and its moons mined via magic technology.

The diameter of Venus was 0.95 times that of the Earth's, and its gravity was 0.9 times that of the Earth's. In this respect, Venus was a more suitable destination for human settlement than Mars. However, Venus's thick carbon dioxide atmosphere, sulfuric acid clouds, and high temperatures, which appeared to be caused by the greenhouse effect, made it difficult to modify the planet's environment. As a result, outer space settlement projects had all moved to Mars.

All things considered, apart from its distance from Earth, Venus was a much more preferable destination than Mars, especially considering the negative effects Mars's low gravity had on the human body. The purpose of the Dione Project was therefore to use magic technology to modify Venus's atmosphere, a task which posed a huge challenge when tackled with conventional technology alone.

Edward Clark named nine people in addition to himself who were necessary for the progression of the project. These did not only include scientists, but also Paul Maximillian, the president of Maximillian Devices, and Fredrich Rosen, the president of Rosen Magicraft.

Feasibility of the project aside, it was a good idea to include the heads of the world's two largest magic engineering manufacturers. Nationally recognized strategic magicians and members of the Thirteen Apostles William MacLeod and Igor Andreivich Bezobrazov were also well-known authorities on magic studies. The likelihood of them actually cooperating on the project was low, but it made sense that their names were mentioned.

The reason the Japanese media paid so much attention to this fairly new project—which was no more than a pretty picture at this stage—was because of the tenth person on Edward's list, whose name was never mentioned.

After listing nine names, Edward Clark told the camera, "There is one more technician we would like to have on the project. I can't say his name, since he is still a minor according to the laws of his home country, but he is a Japanese high school student who goes by the name of Taurus Silver."

"Ridiculous."

Tatsuya muttered bitterly to himself on the living room sofa after watching a recording of the morning news. His mornings lately had been far from refreshing. Now this news broadcast had made the morning even more lackluster.

Miyuki gave him a worried look by his side, at a loss for words. She had no idea what to say to Tatsuya at a time like this.

"Sorry, Miyuki," he apologized, sensing her gaze. "I didn't mean to make you worry again."

His usual, collected smile spread across his lips. But suddenly, his face tensed. Tears were streaming down Miyuki's cheeks.

"……"

This time, Tatsuya fell silent.

"I-I'm sorry," she said, quickly wiping the tears away.

Minami quietly handed her a handkerchief from behind.

"Thank you, Minami," Miyuki said quietly. But after accepting the handkerchief, she didn't use it to wipe her tears. Instead, she used it to hide her face.

"Miyuki…?" Tatsuya cautiously called her name.

She slightly lowered the handkerchief just below her eyes. The skin of her face peeping out underneath her bangs had begun to blush crimson.

"M-my apologies," she said, suddenly shy. "I'm so childish for crying like this."

"I don't think you're childish at all," Tatsuya replied. "Could you just tell me what's wrong?"

Miyuki dropped the white handkerchief onto her lap. A bit of redness still lingered on her cheeks and around her eyes.

"Broth…" She lowered her eyes shyly as she quickly corrected herself. "Tatsuya, I never want you to feel compelled to smile around me."

"I don't—" Tatsuya began, but he couldn't bring himself to complete the excuse. He knew he wasn't a good liar in front of Miyuki.

"You've been put in an extremely difficult situation," she continued. "Both of us are aware of that."

"Right…" Tatsuya murmured.

"I might not be able to do anything to help you, but at least share your burden with me. As you know, I am no longer your little sister; we're engaged."

Miyuki peered up into Tatsuya's eyes. Not in a bold way at all,

but in a way that made her seem embarrassed by her own words, even though she had not said anything strange.

Under usual circumstances, anyone would have lost all reason and embraced her tender frame. They may have even begun devouring her brightly tinted lips. *If you can't forget yourself at a time like this, you're probably missing out*, Tatsuya thought as he stared at Miyuki's bashful expression.

While Miyuki had helped ease the mood, she couldn't stop the backlash that was coming Tatsuya's way. In fact, the real hardship was just beginning.

At Miyuki's request, Tatsuya began sharing his burden by putting his current situation in perspective for her.

"The most inconvenient thing about all this," he said, "is they know I'm Taurus Silver. And there's absolutely nothing we can do about it."

"Not even erasing Edward Clark's memory would do any good, would it?" Miyuki commented.

"No," he replied. "We just have to assume the world knows who I really am and deal with this as best we can."

"Is there no way you could accept Edward Clark's offer to join him?"

Tatsuya shook his head. "Absolutely not. Before I could even consider doing that, I would have to investigate the Dione Project to determine Clark's true intentions. On top of that, my current circumstances make it impossible to work for the USNA, even if it may be beneficial to me as a magician."

"What if Aunt Maya approved of you accepting the offer?" Miyuki prompted.

"Not even her approval would make me leave your side," Tatsuya insisted.

Miyuki's eyes brimmed with tears, and she quickly looked away.

Her earlier declaration had made her more acutely aware of Tatsuya in a romantic sense.

Tatsuya didn't show any signs of being flustered by Miyuki's unusual reaction. He realized a little too late that what he had just said would make just about anyone feel embarrassed, whether they were the speaker or the listener. Especially since Miyuki was no longer his younger sister, but his fiancée, her shyness was to be expected. But apologizing at this point would only make things more awkward. Tatsuya decided to act like he hadn't noticed his fiancée quivering with embarrassment.

"Anyway, that's not to say I'm not intrigued by this international nonmilitary magic project," he said. "Let's start by organizing the information we currently have."

"I'd like to see it, too," Miyuki said.

Edward Clark's press release included a summary of the project. Tatsuya began looking over the original text, while Miyuki pulled herself together and glanced over a translation. As soon as Minami set newly brewed cups of tea in front of them, the pair simultaneously raised their eyes from their e-paper displays.

"Interesting. It seems the *Dione* in the project's name is not referring to Saturn's moon, but rather to the Greek goddess," Miyuki remarked.

"Yeah," Tatsuya said. "She was Zeus's wife and Aphrodite's mother. Of course, that's only if we're going by the version of the myth where Aphrodite wasn't born from sea foam."

"Zeus is Jupiter and Aphrodite is Venus," Miyuki pondered. "That means this project aims to be one on par with the gods, reincarnating Venus through Jupiter's resources."

"That sounds about right," Tatsuya agreed. "But I want to believe the project itself has some significance for humanity."

He returned his gaze to the electronic display with a serious look.

The project consisted of four main elements. The first involved using weighting- and acceleration-type magic to launch materials and prefabricated production plants from Earth's surface into space. The most significant challenge when constructing large-scale structures in space was overcoming Earth's gravity. High-propulsion rockets were required to transport massive objects beyond Earth's orbit. Even if the intention was to use extraterrestrial resources, the initial mining and construction machinery needed to be transported from Earth. To achieve this, the plan was not to develop new rockets but to augment existing rockets with weighting- and acceleration-type magic, enabling the transport of large masses into space.

Luckily, there was a precedent for this. Before the war, there had been a plan to set up a platform for hypersonic projectiles in space as an alternative to nuclear strategic weapons. The main challenge this project had faced was the rocket engine propulsion, since a substantial number of projectiles needed to be deployed to function properly as strategic weapons. The cost of developing a high-propulsion rocket engine to transport that much mass had been exorbitant, even under the pretext that they would be replacing nuclear weapons.

To make up for this cost, those in charge of the project had come up with the idea of sending two magicians with the rocket to manage the rocket's gravity and speed with magic. One magician would reduce the gravitational force acting on the entire rocket, including the mass projectile, missile, and launch platform components. The other magician would amplify the acceleration force generated by the rocket's engine. The USNA's predecessor—the USA—had actually launched military satellites that served as missile-launch platforms using this method before.

However, this plan had been abandoned after the completion of the first strategic military satellite. All twelve magicians involved in the six launches to carry thirty missiles and satellite components into orbit had lost their lives in the process.

The worst part was that this hadn't been an accident. Technically, it had been an accident, but it was all too convenient that no one other than the magicians had been killed. Performing magic under conditions where mass and gravity changed significantly over a short period of time, especially with six hundred tons of cargo involved, had put overwhelming mental strain on the magicians that had proved to be fatal.

Fortunately, there was already a solution in place for this issue. It had not yet been proved due to cost, but conducting experiments like this would most likely lead to success. Tatsuya was not concerned about this part of the plan.

The second element involved using magicians to mine the necessary metals from the asteroid belt. The Dione Project required a significant amount of nickel, which could be obtained from M-type asteroids. Other than nickel, the metals required could likely be sourced from space without tapping into Earth-bound resources. However, resource mining in zero-gravity space had its challenges. Namely, it required the consumption of propellants for movement.

The project heads proposed to address this propellant issue by using movement magic for extravehicular activities. This allowed free movement between asteroids and small celestial bodies while the mother ship served as a reference point. If they were willing to have magicians work as miners in distant asteroid belts for extended periods, this seemed to be a promising idea.

The project's third component involved using magic to extract hydrogen from Jupiter, then transporting it to Venus. The aim was to bring water to the waterless Venus and reduce its carbon dioxide through the Sabatier reaction, where hydrogen and carbon dioxide reacted at high temperatures and pressure to produce water and methane. Nickel would then act as a catalyst in this process.

The idea was to deploy tether satellites—or orbital elevators not fixed to the ground—in Venus's orbit. They would then suspend special nickel containers from them. The tether satellites' main body would then receive the hydrogen collected from Jupiter and deliver it to the nickel containers via cable. The high temperatures and pressures on

Venus's surface would naturally use nickel as a catalyst to spark the Sabatier reaction without the need for additional heat or pressure. If enough water was provided to Venus's atmosphere, scientists anticipated that genetically modified algae could eventually be used to produce oxygen.

Through this scheme, they would place magicians in the orbits of Jupiter's and Venus's moons, using movement and acceleration magic to send hydrogen transport ships from Jupiter to Venus.

However, water in vapor form and methane were both greenhouse gases that were much more potent than carbon dioxide in equal amounts. Even if Venus's carbon dioxide levels were reduced, it would continue to heat up. Therefore, the project's fourth component involved using magic to extract ice from one of Jupiter's Galilean moons, Callisto, and shoot it toward Venus to lower the planet's intra-atmosphere temperatures.

The combination of concentrated sulfuric acid and ice would act as a chilling agent. This was expected to effectively cool Venus's atmosphere once enough ice was injected. Even if the production of water through the Sabatier reaction didn't go as planned, the ice-ferrying operation alone might be sufficient to achieve the first phase of Venusian atmospheric modification.

However, both the third and fourth components of the project required the continuous presence of magicians in Jupiter and Venus's satellite orbits. Not only that, but a substantial number of magicians would likely be necessary to overcome Jupiter's gravity and consistently launch transportation ships and giant masses of ice. Moreover, it wouldn't make sense to place just one or two magicians on Venus to fit tether satellites there, so this would also require many magicians. Those magicians would probably not be able to return to Earth for a long time. Interestingly, the same would be true for the second project component, in which magicians would be tasked with mining minerals in space. That was what made Tatsuya realize the truth.

"I knew it…" he murmured with a furrowed brow.

"Is there a problem?" Miyuki asked.

Tatsuya nodded. "There is a chance I may be overthinking this. In fact, I hope that's the case. But this project's purpose seems to be to banish all magicians that pose a threat to people on Earth."

"Banish them to outer space, you mean?" Miyuki asked in disbelief. But there was no sense of panic in her voice. It was almost as if she couldn't conceive of a situation where that would be true. Tatsuya couldn't blame her. Space development had remained stagnant since its interruption by social turmoil caused by global cooling and subsequent war. Ability to conduct manned spaceflight had likewise declined since the beginning of the twenty-first century.

Even the cream-of-the-crop astronauts found it a challenge to fly to space. So the idea of banishing magicians to space didn't seem to make sense.

"On the surface, the project is only about space development, of course," Tatsuya explained. "But the magicians involved clearly won't be able to return to Earth for extended periods of time. Even if they do return, they will probably be sent back to space again as soon as their health allows."

His gaze remained fixed on the electronic display, and he didn't dare to look up.

"Dedicating your life to space development is an honorable way to live if that's someone's choice. But I—"

He cut himself off, sinking into his own thoughts and avoiding all eye contact with Miyuki.

The next day was a Monday. That morning, only about half the students in Class 3-A had arrived at school so far. Not even Miyuki had shown up yet.

The students who had arrived were clustered in groups around the classroom, chatting. They may be studying magic at First High, but at times like these, they were just regular high school students.

Not many of them were discussing the canceled Nine School Competition. It wasn't that it didn't bother them, but they were clearly avoiding the topic. Not only had a member of Class 3-A used Active Air Mine at a previous Nine School Competition, but many students in the class knew they couldn't have won two competitions in a row without Tatsuya. Perhaps the abundance of representatives in the class made it harder to bring up the competition in conversation.

Instead, many students were discussing the American space development program, which had repeatedly been on the news since the day before. Honoka and Shizuku were no exception.

"Do you think it's true, Shizuku?" Honoka asked.

"Think what's true?" Shizuku asked back.

"You know," Honoka pressed. "That Taurus Silver is actually a Japanese high school student."

She wasn't the only one whispering about Taurus Silver's true identity. It fascinated the students that this genius magic engineer was reportedly someone like them.

"Well, we can't rule it out completely," Shizuku replied. "I mean, look at Kichijouji."

Shinkurou Kichijouji was a senior at Third High. He was a well-known figure in the field of magic because of his discovery of one of the Cardinal Codes, and there was hardly anyone who didn't know his name. He was particularly renowned for having carried out this remarkable achievement at the age of thirteen. Although he hadn't accomplished anything significant since, Shinkurou Kichijouji's name fit in perfectly alongside that of Taurus Silver, who had conceived flight magic, which had been one of the three great unsolved problems in the field of weighting magic.

Given Kichijouji was a similar child prodigy, Shizuku reasoned it wouldn't be unusual if Taurus Silver, too, was a high school student at one of the magic high schools.

"Hey, Shizuku…" Honoka said meekly.

The two girls had known each other for a long time. Shizuku knew this was Honoka's way of showing she needed a little push to say what was on her mind.

"What is it?" Shizuku answered compliantly.

"Do you think Taurus Silver might be Tatsuya?" Honoka asked.

"It's possible," Shizuku replied immediately. Honoka stared at her in silence.

"What?" Shizuku asked.

"I just didn't expect you to answer so quickly," Honoka explained.

"I'm just telling you what immediately came to mind," Shizuku said.

"Do you mean to tell me you thought Tatsuya might be Taurus Silver the moment you heard the magic engineer was a high school student?" Honoka asked in awe.

"Yep." Shizuku nodded without hesitation. Perhaps feeling this wasn't a sufficient answer, she paused before adding, "If Taurus Silver really is a Japanese high school student, Tatsuya is the only person I thought could be him."

"You have a point…" Honoka replied thoughtfully. "But then—!"

She couldn't finish her sentence. At that very moment, Miyuki came into the classroom, sealing Honoka's lips.

"Good morning," Miyuki greeted.

"Good morning, Miyuki," Shizuku returned.

Honoka followed suit: "Good morning, Miyuki."

But she couldn't bring herself to ask the student council president if Tatsuya would be going to America, as she feared.

Tatsuya managed to slip into the classroom just before class started. But the arrival of a message on his self-study desk terminal immediately forced him to leave.

"Is something wrong, Tatsuya?" Mizuki asked from the seat beside him. They had been seat neighbors for two years in a row.

"I've been called into the staff room. I'll see you later," he replied.

A look of worry immediately clouded Mizuki's face. This concern quickly spread to Tatsuya's other classmates, who had heard his answer, and they all turned to look at him.

Tatsuya was glad he hadn't told Mizuki the whole truth; he had actually been called into the principal's office.

Principal Momoyama, Vice Principal Yaosaka, and Class 3-E's homeroom teacher Jennifer Smith were all waiting for Tatsuya when he arrived at the office.

Momoyama skipped the pleasantries and jumped straight to the point: "First of all, there is one thing I'd like to clarify. Tatsuya Shiba, are you Taurus Silver?"

"Why do you ask?" Tatsuya replied to the principal's question with another question.

This was rather disrespectful, but Momoyama didn't seem to mind. In fact, he seemed to have anticipated Tatsuya's unwillingness to provide a straightforward response.

"I received a letter from the National Science Agency, NSA, via the USNA Embassy," Momoyama explained. "In fact, an embassy staff member came directly to my home to deliver it."

Momoyama was not only the principal of First High. He was also a national authority on magic education, although he remained a civilian and stayed away from diplomatic relations. It was highly unusual for an embassy staff member to deliver a letter to a civilian, but the news didn't even make Tatsuya bat an eye. Momoyama, too, maintained his composure in front of the impudent eighteen-year-old. But their eyes were locked in a silent staring contest. Vice Principal Yaosaka paled as he watched their inaudible feud.

After a few seconds, Momoyama pulled a white envelope from his desk drawer and set it on top of his desk.

"This is the letter I received," he said. "It's essentially a request that 'Taurus Silver, also known as Mr. Tatsuya Shiba, should participate in the Dione Project.' It seems the NSA has identified you as Taurus Silver and is requesting your participation in this project."

"Principal Momoyama," Tatsuya said slowly, "I am still a high school student studying at this school. I have no intention of stopping my studies midway."

He deliberately ignored the part about him being Taurus Silver, using the pretext of being a studious high school student to refuse participation in the project.

"I believe having one of our school's students invited to a national-level magic project is an honor," Momoyama replied. He paused, fixing an especially intense gaze on Tatsuya.

"I am not alone in this belief," he continued. "The president of the Magic University is of the same opinion. If you agree to participate in the NSA's project, we have agreed to grant you both a high school diploma and the eligibility for admission to the Magic University. If your participation in the project prevents you from attending college classes, we will automatically award you the appropriate number of credits based on the duration of your project participation. Once four years have passed, we are even more than happy to bestow you with a college degree."

"Is that an official decision?" Tatsuya asked.

"Not yet," Momoyama replied. "But I personally guarantee it. You have my word."

He turned to Jennifer before Tatsuya could speak.

"Ms. Smith, I believe Shiba already possesses the knowledge and skills equivalent to those needed to graduate from our school. Wouldn't you agree?"

"Well, yes," she reluctantly replied. "His stellar reactor experiment even demonstrates he has already reached the level of a Magic University graduate."

"I see."

Momoyama nodded and turned back to Tatsuya. "Shiba, I'm sure you wouldn't want to waste your time in classes at a lower level than your abilities."

"I don't see my time here as a waste at all," Tatsuya said.

"Please. Don't be modest." Momoyama brushed off the teenager's comment and sat up in his chair. "I understand you may not want to rush your decision. Lucky for you, the NSA has not set a deadline for your response. From today onward, we will excuse you from your classes so you can take your time to think it over."

"Does this mean you're putting me under house arrest?" Tatsuya asked slowly.

"Don't get me wrong," Momoyama said nonchalantly. "This isn't some kind of punishment. You're still more than welcome to use our school's facilities as usual. All I'm saying is that you will be treated as if you have completed your coursework, including any practical training. You won't need to take any of your regular exams and all your classes will be processed with a final A grade."

He made it sound as if he was doing Tatsuya some kind of favor.

Seeing there was no room for argument, Tatsuya replied, "Fine. I'll think about it."

The most he could do was to buy some time.

Tatsuya returned to class from the principal's office as if nothing had happened. His last morning class was a practical training session. Ignoring Jennifer's suspicious glances, he participated with the same nonchalant expression as always.

It was not until the beginning of student council activities that Tatsuya's behavior suddenly changed.

"Miyuki, do you have a minute?" he asked.

"Of course," she said. "Do you mind if we talk here?"

"Yes, that's fine. I'd like everyone to hear this."

Not understanding what was going on, Miyuki was somewhat perplexed, but she decided to hear her Tatsuya out. She moved from her desk to the student council's conference table.

Tatsuya sat directly across from her. Meanwhile, Honoka, Izumi, and Shiina turned toward the couple in their seats, and Minami stood behind Miyuki's chair. Pixie, who was sitting in a chair in the corner of the room, got up to prepare tea. From his seat, Tatsuya had a clear view of Minami's unchanged stoic expression. Miyuki waited for Pixie to set the tea in front of them before speaking.

"So what did you want to talk about?" she asked.

Everyone leaned forward to ensure they didn't miss a word of what Tatsuya had to say.

"This morning, the principal called me to his office to tell me I'm exempt from classes," he revealed.

"But why?!" Miyuki immediately paled and jumped from her seat. Honoka was right behind her.

"I'll explain when we get home," Tatsuya said. "He said it's not a suspension or disciplinary action, but they probably don't want me attending school for a while."

"Do you think the school is trying to avoid attracting public attention?" Miyuki asked, returning to her seat and trying to stay calm.

"Yeah."

"...Don't tell me this has something to do with the Nine School Competition," Shizuku spoke up.

"It's not directly connected, but it's probably all related," Tatsuya replied.

Honoka, who was still standing, spoke up next: "Then the direct reason must be—"

This was neither a question nor a soliloquy. She had clearly caught on that the USNA had invited him onto their project because he was Taurus Silver. While she was correct, she pulled back when she locked eyes with Tatsuya.

"N-never mind," she said, shaking her head.

Not wanting to make her uncomfortable, Tatsuya turned back to Miyuki and continued, "Our family might have something to say about this."

Everyone in the room knew he meant the Yotsuba clan.

"I probably won't be able to come to school for a while," he said, "so I'd like you to accept my resignation from the student council."

The entire room fell silent. As Tatsuya patiently waited for Miyuki's reply, Izumi's eyes were on Miyuki, and Honoka's were on Tatsuya. Shiina awkwardly glanced between the two, and Minami stood as still as a statue with her eyes closed.

Pixie retracted the cups of cold tea in front of Miyuki and Tatsuya, followed by Minami quickly replacing the cups with new ones. Then, with a satisfied smile, Miyuki's guard returned to her position.

"All right," Miyuki finally replied with a strained voice. "However, if you step down from the student council, you won't be allowed to carry your CAD on school grounds. It might be better for you to stay on as a student council officer, even if only in name."

"But that won't provide me any sense of closure," Tatsuya argued.

"I won't allow anyone to say anything to you," Miyuki insisted. Naturally, Tatsuya was inclined to tell her she shouldn't be mixing her personal feelings with professional matters. But seeing she was on the verge of tears and filled with desperation, he stood down.

"Fine," he relented. "We'll do things your way."

To tell the truth, he could care less about the school's order at this point.

Reaching closure over the student council was dismissed as a trivial matter, but there were other problems Tatsuya and Miyuki could not brush aside. The letter from the NSA to Principal Momoyama, for example, was one Tatsuya had to tell his aunt about. He carefully chose the right timing and made a call to the main house.

"Hello, Aunt Maya," Tatsuya greeted his aunt over videophone. "Sorry to disturb you so late at night."

"I don't mind," she replied. *"I'm sure it's something urgent."*

Maya's expression made Tatsuya slightly uneasy, because it was clear she wasn't acting; she genuinely didn't know why Tatsuya had called. Careful not to reveal his surprise, he made sure to answer Maya's questions even more thoughtfully than usual.

"Yes, very urgent," he said slowly, and he began to explain the situation before his aunt could speak. "You see, First High's Principal Momoyama, Vice Principal Yaosaka, and Ms. Jennifer Smith have discovered Taurus Silver's true identity. It was written on a letter delivered to the principal from the NSA via the USNA Embassy."

There was a pause before Maya asked, *"Was the letter about that project?"*

Tatsuya's news had clearly come as a surprise.

"Yes," Tatsuya replied.

"I'm sure you didn't admit to it, of course," Maya said. She was confident Tatsuya would never admit he was Taurus Silver.

"I didn't," he replied, "but the cat is practically already out of the bag."

He knew Momoyama and Yaosaka would believe the NSA before they believed him, and they weren't alone. Many people who knew Tatsuya would believe the NSA's statement that he was Taurus Silver. This was not because the NSA was an American political organization, but because Tatsuya had already shown much too much of what he was capable of.

"Right…" Maya said pensively. *"That puts us a little ahead of schedule, but it seems we'll have to give up on Taurus Silver altogether."*

Tatsuya waited as his aunt sorted through her thoughts.

After a few seconds, she asked, *"Did Principal Momoyama say anything else?"*

Tatsuya explained everything Momoyama had told him.

"It seems the principal is trying to get you out of the school to avoid

politicians and the media interfering in First High's management," Maya mused.

"Yes, I thought the same thing," Tatsuya agreed, pleased their speculations aligned.

"Hmm… You may be better off not attending school for a while," Maya advised.

"Are you suggesting a voluntary suspension?" Tatsuya asked.

After Tatsuya had used Material Burst during the Yokohama Incident, Maya had directly ordered him to voluntarily take a break from school at the main house. He wondered if a similar type of punishment awaited him this time as well. But she shook her head.

"I'm not trying to punish you," she assured. *"I just feel that the rumors against you are going to get more intense from now on. I doubt they would faze you, but I'm sure they will be bothersome. So why not pretend to suspend yourself from school and let things calm down a bit?"*

In all honesty, this recommendation didn't sit well with Tatsuya. He couldn't shake the feeling there was more to his aunt's words than met the eye, although he couldn't pinpoint exactly what it was. Of course there were times when avoiding a situation could be effective in resolving a problem. Rather than enduring the noise and possibly submitting to it, taking a step back could spark some kind of change. But there was one vital sacrifice that would need to be made no matter what.

"Your break from school does not have to happen right away," Maya continued. *"Since you will be away from Miyuki for a while, it is important we make some necessary arrangements first."*

That was precisely what Tatsuya had been thinking. Although Tatsuya had been exempted from attending school, he couldn't take Miyuki out of school with him.

Tatsuya had taken absences from school for up to about a week before, but this time, he might be gone for over a month. It was perfectly possible to watch over her from afar, but the idea of leaving Miyuki and Minami alone in their house for so long put Tatsuya on edge.

Maya glanced at Miyuki at Tatsuya's side and Minami, who was standing diagonally behind them, before turning her gaze back to Tatsuya.

"While you may not like this, Tatsuya, I would like to leave Minami in charge of Miyuki's security at school," she said, to which Tatsuya shook his head.

"I'm perfectly fine with that," he said. "I have full confidence in Minami's abilities."

A faint blush tinged Minami's cheeks. Her heart swelled with excitement to hear Tatsuya trusted her wholeheartedly.

"All right, then," Maya said. *"We're counting on you, Minami."*

"Leave it to me, ma'am," Minami replied with resolve.

Maya gave her a satisfied nod and continued: *"We will arrange for someone on our end to accompany you to and from school. This does not mean I question your abilities, Minami. I just do not want to leave anything to chance."*

Minami nodded solemnly. "Of course."

She wasn't arrogant enough to insist on handling everything on her own.

"The issue is at night," Maya continued. *"While there may be two of you in the house, it is still possible something may happen while you sleep."*

Tatsuya, Miyuki, and Minami didn't dare dispute their aunt's words. Even though they believed there was no need to worry deep down, they knew better than to risk making Maya angry.

"Miyuki."

"Yes, Aunt Maya?"

"I know this is asking a lot, but would you mind moving to Chofu?"

This was clearly a measure particularly for Miyuki's safety.

"By Chofu, do you mean that tall building with the shutters?" Miyuki asked.

"That's the one." Maya nodded with a smile. *"It was constructed to be the Yotsuba family's metropolitan headquarters. The plan has always been*

for you to move there eventually. Extenuating circumstances have simply pushed up the schedule of that plan. I would like you to move there this Sunday. We will take care of the necessary arrangements."

This was all too sudden for Miyuki. But she knew she couldn't go against her aunt's wishes.

"Understood," she responded quietly.

"Excellent. After Miyuki moves, I would like Tatsuya to go to our Izu villa for a while," Maya instructed.

"The Yotsuba family has a headquarters in Izu?" Tatsuya asked. He thought the main house would be a better place for him, but he didn't dare voice his opinion and risk stirring up trouble.

"I'm surprised you don't know about it," Maya said in mock surprise.

Hearing the sarcasm in her voice, Tatsuya decided to wait to hear what his aunt said.

Sure enough, his aunt continued, *"The villa in Izu is where my sister, your mother, underwent medical care."*

"I thought you would have disposed of it by now," Tatsuya said.

"Of course not," Maya replied. *"It was your mother's favorite villa."*

Tatsuya didn't think the Yotsuba family would be sentimental enough to save a place like that, but he quickly reconsidered. For the sake of a single girl, they had challenged the nation and traded half their lives for revenge. In that sense, a degree of sentimentality made sense.

"We will have everything you need moved in by next Sunday," Maya added. *"We will even set up some research equipment, so you do not need to bring a thing."*

Having all the workstations and calibration equipment set up in a single week seemed too good to be true. Tatsuya couldn't help but suspect the villa in Izu was used as a research outpost, not just as a personal retreat. But he kept these thoughts to himself.

"As you wish," he said with an obedient bow.

After the call with Tatsuya ended, Maya's smile twisted into a displeased frown. She downed the contents of her teacup like it was a bitter medicine and began to return it to her desk. But just before the cup touched the saucer, Maya threw it into the air. Suddenly, the room became a dazzling nightscape. It wasn't that darkness had fallen. The air was full of twinkling stars, shooting across the sky in all directions. As the nightscape faded away, teacup fragments dropped to the floor, sparkling under the room lights.

"Someone clean up this mess." Hayama's calm voice resonated behind Maya.

"Right away," a maid in uniform replied, obediently carrying over a broom and dustpan.

She carefully swept the floor of every single teacup fragment before retreating out of the room. Once she was gone, Hayama moved into Maya's field of vision.

"Shall I bring you more tea, ma'am?" he asked.

"No need," Maya replied. None of the frustration that had led her to cast Meteor Line lingered in her voice.

"It seems the USNA got the best of us this time," Hayama commented.

"Yes," Maya reluctantly replied. "As you said, I relied too much on Hlidskjalf. I suppose this is what happens the moment the system goes down."

Her lips twisted into a wry smile.

"On the contrary, ma'am," Hayama consoled. "I believe that even if we had known in advance what they were planning this time, there was no way to prevent it. Even our influence does not reach the USNA's national agencies."

"Surely, we could have at least assassinated Edward Clark," Maya joked darkly.

"Lingering in the hypothetical will get us nowhere, ma'am," Hayama replied.

"True," Maya sighed. "I shouldn't say things I don't really mean."

Even if it had been possible, the truth of the matter was that the Yotsuba family never would have issued an order for an assassination. At this point, wishful thinking about it was pointless.

"I believe we should prioritize thinking about the very fact that Hlidskjalf did come to a stop," Hayama suggested.

Maya glanced at him with marginal surprise. "Are you saying there is a connection between Edward Clark and Hlidskjalf?"

"Hlidskjalf is the hacking system for the global communications-interception system, Echelon III," Hayama explained. "It's quite conceivable that NSA personnel may be involved in its shutdown."

"Hmm. I don't think that directly changes the current situation, but it is definitely something to keep in mind," Maya mused, to which Hayama respectfully bowed.

[4]

The next morning, after an intense sparring session, Tatsuya told Yakumo he wanted to take a break from training for a while.

"That's fine," Yakumo replied. "You're not really my disciple anyway, so you can quit anytime. We can spar whenever I'm free."

"Thank you, Master."

Even though Tatsuya wasn't his disciple, he still found it natural to call Yakumo his master. Yakumo didn't scold or correct him. His lips didn't even twist into a wry smile.

"That said," he continued, "I would still like to hear why you want to take a break. Does it have something to do with the American space development plan?"

Yakumo's face filled with curiosity. Tatsuya almost chuckled, but the impulse to laugh immediately vanished. The situation he was facing was anything but funny, so he didn't really feel like laughing.

"Yes, that's the primary cause," Tatsuya said. "I'll be on academic suspension for a while at the Yotsuba family's villa in Izu."

Despite Maya saying otherwise, Tatsuya still thought this period felt like a suspension. He added that his household would be moving to Chofu.

"I see," Yakumo remarked. "That means you'll be farther away."

"It's still commutable," Tatsuya said. "If it's okay, I'd like to continue training with you once my suspension is over."

"Of course," Yakumo replied immediately. Then he fell into thought before adding, "But aren't you worried about Miyuki? While I'm sure the distance between Izu and Chofu won't be a problem for you, it's not as if you can travel between the two in an instant."

"Admittedly, I am worried," Tatsuya said. "But Miyuki can't afford to skip school."

"Well, I'm sure the Yotsuba family has arranged additional security for her," Yakumo mused, "but not many people are at your level. Since this whole fiasco seems like it will take some time to resolve, how about I keep an eye out for her, too?"

"That would be amazing," Tatsuya said. "But why would you do all that for me?"

As established earlier, he wasn't Yakumo's disciple. That made Yakumo and Miyuki nothing more than acquaintances. Although the two were relatively close, Tatsuya couldn't help but wonder if there was something more that made Yakumo want to help.

However, he immediately regretted asking. Yakumo's lips curled into a smile as if he had been waiting for the opportunity to answer this very question.

"I'm not ready to die yet, you see," he said.

"What is that supposed to mean?" Tatsuya asked.

"If something were to happen to Miyuki, you would surely end up destroying the world," Yakumo explained. "I may be powerful, but I doubt I could survive flames stronger than a nuclear bomb."

Tatsuya was at a loss for words. If something were to happen to Miyuki again and he couldn't intervene in time, he didn't have the confidence to say he would quietly accept fate. Without question, he would try to do something to make the world pay for taking Miyuki from him.

◇ ◇ ◇

That day, Tatsuya didn't make an appearance in the classroom. He arrived at school but decided to hole up in the library all day without even a break for lunch. The only time he left was to meet up with Miyuki after school.

His friends didn't dare go near him. Even Erika didn't bother the couple on their way home from school like she usually did. Only Minami followed behind them.

The next day and the day after that were much the same.

That Thursday after school, a group of First High students were gathered on a nearby café terrace thirty minutes before closing time.

"I'm worried about him," Erika suddenly said.

"You mean Tatsuya?" Mikihiko asked.

Erika shot him a look as if it was obvious. "Duh. Don't you think he's missing too much class lately?"

"I heard the principal excused all his absences for the rest of the year," Leo said.

Honoka, who had joined the group after her student council duties were over, nodded. Even she had trouble interrupting Tatsuya and Miyuki when they were together nowadays.

"Well, that doesn't sound good," Shizuku interjected.

Mizuki looked confused. "Why do you say that, Shizuku?"

"It means Tatsuya doesn't have a reason to come to school anymore," Shizuku replied bluntly. Her total lack of unnecessary embellishments clearly reflected the dire situation at hand.

A look of shock came over Mizuki's face, and she covered her mouth with both hands. Honoka cast her eyes downward with a pained expression. But not only seniors were present at the table. Kasumi, who Izumi had coerced into joining the gathering, looked uncomfortable in her chair.

"Are you saying he won't *ever* come back to school?" she asked now, daring to verbalize what no one else seemed willing to say.

"Well, I'm sure he'll come back once things settle down," Shizuku replied.

"O-of course he will!" Honoka exclaimed, desperately trying to cling to hope.

"Will things ever settle down?" Erika spat in frustration. Her words added fuel to the fire. Or maybe they were more like icicles, since they froze Honoka's expression in place.

"Erika!" Mikihiko scolded. "Don't say things like that!" Although he wasn't that loud, everyone could sense the raw anger in his voice.

"Cool it, Mikihiko," Leo warned. "You have to admit Erika has a point. I can't see the situation cooling off within the next couple of months."

"I know that!" Mikihiko spat back. "But she doesn't have to say it out loud."

"Because Mizuki and Mitsui might be traumatized? I don't think you have to worry about that," Leo said. He was trying to defend Erika, yet she was the first to snap back.

"Do you mean you don't care if Tatsuya never comes back to school?" she asked.

"It's not that I don't care," Leo explained. "I just think it doesn't change the fact that we're his friends."

Erika blinked in silence. Honoka and Mizuki followed suit.

"Wow, I could never be like you," Erika whispered without any trace of malice.

"Is that supposed to be a compliment?" Leo asked suspiciously.

"Who knows?" Erika said with an ambiguous shrug. "I'm just stating facts."

"Why you little—"

"Cut it out, Leo," Mikihiko intervened. "Now it's your turn to cool it."

Suddenly, Izumi spoke up, breaking the tension among Erika, Leo, and Mikihiko.

"Saijou," she said, "I really admire your friendship. But I don't want Tatsuya to leave school."

Both Kasumi and Shiina looked at Izumi in surprise.

"His absence will only make Miyuki sad," she continued.

Of course, Kasumi sighed to herself, feeling foolish that she hadn't seen it coming. *Everything always comes back to Miyuki.*

"That's it!" Shizuku exclaimed.

"What's it?" Honoka puzzled.

"Miyuki won't stay in school if Tatsuya drops out," Shizuku predicted.

Izumi immediately paled.

"I don't think Tatsuya would want Miyuki to drop out, either," she began. Then her face suddenly lit up. "Wait, you're right! Tatsuya would do anything for Miyuki!"

"Exactly." Shizuku nodded enthusiastically. "He would even stay in school."

"But wouldn't something have to change about the current situation for that to happen?" Saburou said cautiously.

The positivity of the table suddenly dropped. Shiina shot her childhood friend an angry stare, making him shrink in his chair. As the unintentional silence dragged on, the awkwardness worsened. Just then, the coffee shop's monitor switched to the news.

"Is that…for real?" Leo whispered.

No one complained about the sudden broadcast—perhaps because they were all curious to see it. The monitor displayed a prerecorded broadcast from Moscow featuring a high-ranking official from the New Soviet Academy and Igor Andreivich Bezobrazov, a strategic magician and a member of the Thirteen Apostles.

The coverage shifted to an interview with Bezobrazov himself.

"Dr. Bezobrazov," the interviewer began, "could you please tell us why you have chosen to participate in the American Dione Project?"

"As I said before, I believe the terraforming of Venus holds a significance that transcends international squabbles. For over a century, humanity has been haunted by the looming danger of overpopulation.

This fear could lead to catastrophic conflicts and an irreversible decline in our civilization's dynamism in the not too distant future. Securing more habitats for humanity is perhaps the only solution to the impending crisis that threatens our future."

"Is this why you have been so proactive about being part of the project?" the interviewer asked.

"Why, yes," Bezobrazov said. "Magic should be used to forge the future of humanity, rather than employed as a weapon of conflict among human beings."

"Once the project progresses to a practical stage," the interviewer continued, "there may arise a time when you will need to leave the New Soviet Union and relocate your base of operations to the United States. That naturally poses two questions: Has the government granted their approval for such a scenario? And given your role as a strategic magician, how are concerns about national defense in your potential extended absence being addressed?"

"Our government cherishes peace," Bezobrazov explained, "and, therefore, has assured me of its full cooperation with the project, even if that means a degree of cutting back our national defense. However, the question of where to establish my research base is a delicate matter and remains undecided."

"Does that mean there is a possibility your base could be right here in the New Soviet Union?" the interviewer asked.

"Of course," Bezobrazov nodded. "However, I personally believe it is even more likely the new base will be established in a neutral country free from political control."

"Fascinating," the interviewer commented. "I'm sure choosing this location alone will generate considerable contention."

"To be sure, this is an unprecedented and grand undertaking in human history," Bezobrazov said. "Various challenges await us. Determining the project's base is only one of them. However, we believe resolution will come through the power of reason. For this reason, we invite not only those who have already announced their participation, such as Sir William MacLeod and Mr. Maximillian, but also newcomers, such as Fredrich Rosen and the Japanese youth known as Taurus Silver, to join this project. Together, we will combine our strengths and overcome all difficulties for the future of humanity."

"Dr. Bezobrazov, thank you for your time."

At this point, the program shifted to an overview of the Dione Project. The students, who had been staring intently at the footage, shifted their gazes away from the monitor.

Erika was the first to speak.

"Like hell his government cherishes peace. Give me a break," she spat angrily.

She was referencing the Sado Island invasion five years ago. Armed forces had launched a surprise attack on Sado Island while the Great Asian Alliance invaded Okinawa. While a volunteer army led by the Ichijou family had managed to repel the attack, the common belief was that the New Soviet Union had orchestrated the whole thing.

The country had never assumed responsibility for the incident, but few Japanese citizens believed the New Soviet Union was innocent. Given this background, Erika's reaction to Bezobrazov's statement that "the New Soviet Union cherished peace" was understandable to say the least.

"Sure, the New Soviet Union may have a laundry list of offenses, but you have to admit Dr. Bezobrazov's statement was persuasive," Mikihiko said.

He didn't think Erika was wrong, but he believed it was important to separate the current issue from past events.

"On a different note, it's pretty bold for a strategic magician to leave the country for nonmilitary purposes," Kasumi commented.

"That's why it's so convincing. The New Soviet Union is striking a new pose, claiming to be serious about their desire to use magic peacefully," Izumi remarked with a hint of sarcasm.

"You might call it a pose," Leo said with a wry smile that quickly twisted into a grave frown. "But Bezobrazov—a New Soviet Union citizen—is still participating in an American project. Who knows if he's really committed or not, but the fact remains that the New Soviet Union has long been an enemy of the United States. If those two nations are cooperating, it makes it awkward for Japan—a USNA ally—to refuse to join the project."

"That's true," Shizuku murmured.

"I'm sure that means the Magic Association would want Taurus Silver to declare his participation voluntarily," Mikihiko added.

"I hope Tatsuya will be okay," Honoka whispered solemnly.

Saburou and Shiina, who had not yet recognized Taurus Silver was Tatsuya, exchanged puzzled glances with question marks practically visible over their heads.

Tatsuya had left school a bit earlier than his friends, accompanied by Miyuki and Minami. As soon as they returned home, they watched the prerecorded news. Once it was over, Miyuki spoke.

"Was that really Bezobrazov, a member of the Thirteen Apostles?" she asked.

Strategic magicians tended to hide their identities to avoid assassinations or other threats on their lives. It seemed counterintuitive for one to appear on public television for all to see.

"It could be a body double," Tatsuya replied. He didn't find it strange at all for Bezobrazov to appear on television at a time like this, but he couldn't take any news from the New Soviet Union at face value.

"Then again," he continued, "it doesn't really matter if he was the real thing or a fake."

"What do you mean?" Miyuki asked.

Tatsuya met her gaze before rewinding the interview and playing it from the beginning.

"The most important issue here is that the New Soviet Union is announcing they'll be cooperating with the USNA's plan," he explained while staring intently at the interview's subtitles. "The Great Asian Alliance and Indo-Persian Federation are formidable powers, but contemporary geopolitics still revolve around the rivalry between the United States and the New Soviet Union. After the Global War Outbreak, the modern international community has centered itself around the competition between the resurgent New Soviet Union and the increasingly powerful USNA."

"I can understand that much," Miyuki replied.

She had taken international relations courses in middle school, and the fact that she was an exemplary student meant she was well-versed in the subject.

"Well, the New Soviet Union has made the Dione Project an exception to the power struggle on the international stage," Tatsuya said. "Whether they contribute to the project or not isn't particularly relevant at this stage. The fact that a USNA adversary has declared they'll be participating means the USNA's allies can no longer ignore the Dione Project. It might even be possible the two nations are scheming together for this very reason."

His conclusion aligned with Leo's and Mikihiko's. However, his extra speculation at the end added a bit of a personal touch.

"But why would the USNA and New Soviet Union join forces?" Miyuki inquired curiously.

She didn't react negatively to Tatsuya's speculation itself. In fact, her fiancé's opinion meant more to her than common sense.

"The USNA and New Soviet Union overwhelmingly dominate other nations in terms of quantity and quality of their conventional forces," Tatsuya explained. "The GAA was catching up for a while, but they haven't fully recovered from the damage they suffered two years ago."

While he spoke about this incident neutrally, he himself was responsible for the significant blow to the Great Asian Alliance's fleet.

He continued: "Magic is equivalent to personal power, but conventional military strength is equivalent to the power of a nation backed by political and economic forces. Now that nuclear weapons are banned, economic strength has become increasingly influential. Unfortunately, smaller countries with limited economies can't effectively counter the USNA and New Soviet Union via conventional means. Japan is no exception to this rule."

"I wouldn't necessarily call Japan a small country," Miyuki countered.

"Well, it definitely can't compare with the New Soviet Union's military or economy," Tatsuya gently refuted. "The world has managed to maintain its current structure without being completely swallowed by great powers thanks to magic. But without magical weapons, small countries wouldn't stand a chance. That's why it's impossible to reject the military's use of magic completely."

Tatsuya's ultimate goal was to limit magic to nonmilitary use and liberate magicians from their role as cogs in the military system. Acknowledging the importance of magical weapons was undoubtedly a hard pill for him to swallow.

"So is the USNA and New Soviet Union's goal to gather powerful magicians through the Dione Project to deprive other countries of their magical strengths?" Miyuki asked, ignoring Tatsuya's last phrase. While not entirely, she understood his conflicted feelings on the matter to some extent.

"That would make sense," Tatsuya murmured, and he fell deep into thought.

Miyuki's question made him aware of a flaw in his own plan and issues he hadn't considered before. The fundamental concept of liberating magicians from being tools of war was undoubtedly reasonable. The reality of magicians being used as expendable weapons should not be endorsed.

However, what if the advancement of the economic use of magic led to a shortage of high-level magicians in the military? What if the cost-effective and highly powerful weapon that was magic completely disappeared? Wouldn't this cause small countries to lose their ability to resist the influence of larger nations? Tatsuya hated to imagine a future where the world became divided and ruled by a few major powers, leading to worldwide conflicts once again.

Maybe deterrence is still necessary, he thought.

The ultimate weapon of mass destruction lay at his disposal. Regardless of how the future unfolded, was it inevitable for him to bear the stigma of possessing such power?

It may have been this very evening that convinced him to make up his mind.

Across the Atlantic, a top secret teleconference guarded by Echelon III subsystems took place in the late hours of the night, Japan time. Bezobrazov started off the conversation.

"Sir MacLeod," he said, "it has been far too long. I believe the last time we spoke was five years ago."

"Indeed it was," MacLeod replied. "Good to see you, old chap. But I must correct you as I did all those years ago. I may have been knighted, but you need not call me 'sir.'"

It was hard to tell if he was serious, stubborn, or simply making a poorly timed joke.

"Do you really have to be so formal?" Clark interrupted, clearly not understanding the humor. "This isn't an official meeting, so let him call you Sir MacLeod if he wants."

His gentle chiding was simply meant to prevent Bezobrazov from getting offended and disrupting the meeting.

"Thank you for your concern, Dr. Clark," Bezobrazov responded cordially. "I don't believe we've formally met."

"Right," the American responded. "Nice to meet you, Dr. Bezobrazov. I'm Edward Clark."

At this point, all three men had finished their introductions.

"I'd like to jump straight to business, Dr. Clark," Bezobrazov began abruptly. "Is it true this Great Bomb you speak of belongs to the strategic magician Taurus Silver, and he is actually a Japanese high school student?"

"That's correct," Clark replied. "We call the spell *Great Bomb*, but its official Japanese name is Material Burst. From what we can tell, it converts mass directly into energy."

"Directly, you say?" Bezobrazov repeated with wonder.

"Fascinating," MacLeod said before cautioning, "However, there is no need to discuss the spell's mechanisms here and now."

"Of course," Bezobrazov admitted. "There is no point in bringing up theoretical concepts when we lack the data to prove it."

"Material Burst is much like your Tuman Bomba, Dr. Bezobrazov," Clark continued. "We believe it can target the entire Earth based on reconnaissance satellite data."

MacLeod nodded firmly. "That certainly poses a threat to the global military balance."

Bezobrazov ignored Clark's insinuation that he understood the mechanisms of Tuman Bomba.

MacLeod continued, "I'm not aware how far Material Burst can reach, but surely it can't reach Earth from Jupiter's orbit."

Bezobrazov turned to Clark and asked, "Is your plan to exile Taurus Silver to Jupiter's orbit?"

"Yes," Clark nodded. "The Dione Project's Ganymede stage has been devised while taking into consideration Taurus Silver's achievements. I'd like him to dedicate the rest of his life to the future of humanity on Ganymede."

"Dr. Clark, you must tell me who Taurus Silver truly is," Bezobrazov insisted.

"I'll tell you once we meet face-to-face," Clark said.

"Fine," Bezobrazov relented. "Then I will look forward to it."

"Where will the meeting take place?" MacLeod asked.

"On the Atlantic Ocean. I thought it would be in all our best interests to avoid any political entanglements," Clark explained.

"Will all three nations rendezvous via ship?" Bezobrazov asked.

"We have already designated the Enterprise as our official meeting location. Both of you will be arriving either via ship or aircraft," Clark explained.

"The Enterprise?" Bezobrazov murmured with interest. "You don't say."

The Enterprise was a new USNA aircraft carrier that had inherited a storied name. Despite not running on nuclear power, the carrier was rumored to have output and endurance comparable to vessels that did, garnering worldwide attention for its mystery system.

"All right," Bezobrazov assented. "I will arrive by air."

"And I will do the same," MacLeod echoed.

"Excellent," Clark said. "Now, there are just a few more things I'd like to cover before we end this meeting."

The teleconference continued for about thirty more minutes under Clark's lead.

Since the April uprising in Mexico, there had been several small-scale riots in the USNA. However, the situation had not yet escalated to the point that called for a military response. Espionage activities against Japan continued at a reduced scale, but there were no major ongoing operations outside the country.

Meanwhile, the USNA's Joint Staff Headquarters for the Stars had scheduled training sessions. On her way to the cafeteria after finishing morning exercises, Lina was stopped by a junior officer and escorted to the commander's office.

"Major Sirius, at your service," she announced at the door.

Dressed in her Angie Sirius disguise, Lina saluted Colonel Paul Walker, the commander of the base. Although Lina was the Stars commander, Colonel Walker was still the highest-ranking official on this base and oversaw the Stars's combat magicians.

"I have orders from Joint Staff Headquarters," Walker said.

"Yes, sir," Lina replied, dropping her salute and standing formally before her superior.

"They would like you to fly to Washington D.C. to join Dr. Edward Clark," Walker relayed. "Then you will act as Clark's bodyguard and report to the Enterprise currently deployed in the Atlantic."

"Yes, sir," Lina repeated.

Walker continued. "Aboard the Enterprise, you will attend a top secret meeting regarding the Dione Project. The other participants include William MacLeod and Bezobrazov the Igniter."

Lina's face suddenly filled with a mixture of both surprise and understanding. Even though it was on the high seas, the idea of a strategic magician from another country boarding a military ship was hard to believe. However, if the participants were members of the Thirteen Apostles, it only made sense that the presence of Lina, who was also a Thirteen Apostle, would be necessary to balance things out.

"As I'm sure you already know, this meeting must be kept top secret," Walker stressed.

"Y-yes. Of course, sir," Lina quickly replied.

While the United States, the United Kingdom, and the New Soviet Union advanced their plans, Japan saw its own share of bustling activity. Unfortunately, this activity was not done because they wanted to do it; they were essentially being forced into it by international pressure.

It had become a custom for a member of the Hundred Families' Numbers to assume the position of president of the Magic Association of Japan. Elections were held every June, and the new president took office in July. While there were no limits on how many times an individual could be elected, no one ever served for more than three years since it was not a particularly lucrative position.

The current president, who had taken office the summer prior, was Hisui Tomitsuka, the biological mother of Hagane Tomitsuka. Even though she was a widow, the Tomitsuka family was not exclusively matrilineal.

The president of the Magic Association of Japan was required to be stationed at the headquarters in Kyoto. The Tomitsuka family, however, was based in the eastern Tokyo Bay area. Consequently, the Tomitsuka male head traditionally managed the family business while the female head oversaw the affairs of the Magic Association.

Hisui Tomitsuka had taken the position of president with a casual mindset, believing it would simply be a temporary role. Now, however, she found herself cursing her past decision.

When American Edward Clark had first announced the Dione Project, it hadn't felt like an immediate threat. In fact, Hisui had assumed it would be difficult for the USNA to invite magicians from abroad. Moreover, the idea of borrowing another country's Thirteen Apostles member seemed impossible. Hisui wasn't the only one who had thought this; all the Magic Association of Japan staff had agreed.

However, this had all changed when Igor Bezobrazov, a member of the Thirteen Apostles and citizen of a major rival nation to the United States, had declared his intent to participate. Now any leniency that might have existed for other nations had instantly been reduced to zero.

Originally, there had been no room for complaint about using magic for the peaceful advancement of humanity's future. Anti-magic activists gained public support by arguing magic was a dangerous weapon that could harm non-magicians.

The use of magic for peaceful purposes—not just minor contributions, like putting out fires or preventing floods, but for grand projects that had profound impacts on humanity's future—was an effective countermeasure against anti-magic statements. Therefore, the Dione Project didn't need to succeed or even materialize; the mere fact it was underway served as a rebuttal to anti-magic movements and provided an opportunity for magicians to overcome their current predicament. However, this also made it impossible for any magician to oppose the project or even put it on hold. The high schooler who went by the name Taurus Silver had to join as soon as possible.

Hisui knew who Taurus Silver was. She had received a hand-delivered letter from the USNA embassy sealed with an old-fashioned wax stamp containing that very information. She lifted her head from her hands. Crying wouldn't solve anything. There was no hero to swoop in and solve her problems for her, and she wasn't in the privileged position to indulge in the feelings of a tragic heroine.

Hisui decided to utilize her authority as the Magic Association of Japan's president to convene a Master Clans Council. Using a special communication line, she called for an online conference with the heads of the Ten Master Clans.

It was quite possible the heads of the Ten Master Clans had anticipated Hisui's call. One hour after they were summoned, the heads of the Ichijou, Futatsugi, Mitsuya, Yotsuba, Itsuwa, Mutsuzuka, Saegusa, Shippou, Yatsushiro, and Juumonji families appeared on Hisui's conference monitor.

"Ms. Yotsuba, thank you so much for your help recently," Gouki Ichijou said suddenly.

"It was my pleasure," Maya replied. "How are you feeling now?"

"Much better, thanks to you," Gouki said with a smile.

"That's wonderful to hear," Mai Futatsugi interrupted, and she turned to Hisui's image on the screen. "So, Ms. President, why have you gathered us here today?"

Despite the rude interlude she had created between Gouki and Maya, Mai's interjection managed to refocus the discussion on Hisui.

Regaining her composure, she greeted, "Hello, everyone. Thank you for taking time out of your busy schedules to join me today on such short notice."

"Well, you did say it was an emergency meeting," Kouichi Saegusa said with a scoff. "Why don't you hurry up and tell us what it's all about?"

Hisui almost burst into tears under the sudden pressure. She was not a particularly weak person, but she was not accustomed to direct confrontation. She preferred to be thoroughly prepared before engaging in any negotiations.

"O-of course," she stammered. Then, taking on her responsibilities as president, she continued. "As I'm sure many of you have already guessed, I wanted to speak about the USNA project that will be happening on Venus. Due to the New Soviet Union's announcement of their participation in the project, the Magic Association of Japan has been forced to respond promptly."

"Why should the association be involved?" Takumi Shippou pointed out in a scholarly tone. "I thought Edward Clark was calling for individual participation."

"Officially, yes," Raizou Yatsushiro responded with a wry smile. "But one of those individuals he personally designated is a Japanese citizen."

"It sounds like an arbitrary decision to me," Atsuko Mutsuzuka retorted with an offended tone. "We have no obligation to comply."

"Unfortunately, it's not that simple," Hisui explained nervously as an array of stern faces glared back at her on the monitor. She took a deep breath, feeling both defiant and determined as she continued.

"Currently, magicians are facing baseless accusations of being enemies of peace. While this is merely childish propaganda on the part of anti-magic activists, the repeated use of strategic magicians and their magic on a global stage lends credibility to their words."

The gazes of the clan heads shifted. Although difficult to tell on the small screen, they were all looking at Maya. Everyone at the meeting recognized Hisui's statement was in part implicitly referring to Tatsuya's Active Air Mine.

Hisui continued unfazed. "Dr. Clark's Dione Project serves as an excellent example of how magic can contribute to humanity beyond military applications. The International Magic Association is even preparing a statement to express their full support. Moreover, I've heard associations in the United States, the United Kingdom, and the New Soviet Union are planning separate press releases to address the project. Germany has been suggesting their participation will not be limited to Rosen Magicraft. Given these developments, Japan cannot afford to be left behind."

"I understand your impatience, Ms. Hisui, but what exactly are we supposed to do? Locate Taurus Silver and force him to participate?" Isami Itsuwa's question came off as reproachful. He had been forced to send his frail daughter to the battlefield before simply because she was a strategic magician. Since then, he harbored a strong aversion to burdening individuals with matters of state just to maintain public appearances.

"Actually, I have already located him," Hisui stated.

Like Itsuwa, she didn't like the idea of sacrificing someone for the sake of appearances. Her feelings, therefore, led to a strange tension, as if she felt the need to bear some of the hardship herself.

"Taurus Silver is Ms. Yotsuba's son," she wrenched out. "Isn't that right?"

Maya gazed at Hisui through the screen, as if questioning her reasoning.

"I received a letter from the American Embassy," Hisui explained. "Considering the person in question is a minor, I would like to refrain from disclosing his name publicly, but I would like all of your assistance in persuading Taurus Silver—Mr. Tatsuya Shiba—to join Dr. Clark's cause."

"Talk about a well-formulated type of coercion," Gouki muttered bitterly.

He wasn't the only one expressing clear resentment. On the other hand, Maya, although the closest to the person in question, was the most composed.

"Principal Momoyama from First High has already discussed this matter with us," she said with a smile. "I will leave the ultimate decision to Tatsuya himself."

Although Hisui was almost the same age as Maya, it took her a few seconds to compose herself and suppress the trembling in her voice.

"Do you mean to say you have no intention of persuading him, Ms. Yotsuba?"

"The project would consume the rest of his life, after all," Maya replied with a friendly, if not elusive tone. "If that is all, would you mind if I take my leave?"

She was clearly not willing to engage in any further questioning.

"Thank you for your time," Hisui said.

"If you'll excuse me, then," Maya said, and she vanished from the screen.

"I'd like to be excused, as well," Atsuko Mutsuzuka echoed, followed by Raizou Yatsushiro.

Now only seven of the ten family heads remained in the virtual meeting.

"The project may be lifelong, but we'd appreciate being able to take some responsibility toward the Japanese magical community," Kouichi Saegusa muttered with a mix of exasperation and resignation.

"Are you suggesting we entirely disregard Tatsuya's will?" Takumi Shippou asked.

"As magicians of the Ten Master Clans, some degree of self-sacrifice is inevitable," Saegusa explained. "Itsuwa, despite physical challenges, your daughter answered the National Defense Force's call and went into battle, did she not?"

"Well, yes…" Itsuwa replied reluctantly. Put that way, it was impossible to refute Saegusa's statement.

"I don't know," Gouki said. "Involving the Yotsuba heir in a foreign-led planetary development project seems like a significant loss for our national defense."

"I'm not sure how much magic he uses exactly, but I think it was this direct link between magicians and military power that put us under fire in the first place," Hisui responded. "Currently, the biggest threats not only to the Japanese magical community but to magicians worldwide are the humanist and anti-magic movements. Dealing with these should be our top priority."

"It's not ideal, but sending Tatsuya Shiba to the United States may be our best option," Mai Futatsugi sighed.

No one opposed her claim.

"But practically speaking, who will persuade him to go?" Gen Mitsuya prompted. "We clearly can't expect much from Ms. Yotsuba in that regard."

His challenging question left even Kouichi silent. Desperate times called for desperate measures.

"Mr. Juumonji," Hisui ventured, "wouldn't you say you have a fairly close personal relationship with Tatsuya?"

Katsuto had simply been Tatsuya's senior at school. He had graduated a year ago and wasn't in the kind of position that would allow him to easily persuade the younger boy. Now, Hisui's son, Hagane, was Tatsuya's classmate and a fellow student at First High. This made Hagane much closer to Tatsuya than Katsuto. Nevertheless, Katsuto volunteered to take on the challenge.

"I don't know if he will listen to me," he said, "but I can give it a try."

"Are you sure?" Kouichi asked.

"All I can do is talk to him," Katsuto said. "I can't promise any results."

None of the remaining family heads could discern his true intentions behind agreeing to negotiate with Tatsuya.

[5]

"It's all a little sad," Miyuki whispered as she stepped out through the small gate of their typical residential home.

"It's not like we're selling it. We can return anytime," Tatsuya reassured her.

"Yes, you're right," Miyuki said.

"I'm sorry to rush you, but are you ready to leave?" a polite voice asked behind them.

Tatsuya spun around to find the young Hyougo Hanabishi waiting for them in a black suit and white gloves.

"Yes, we are," he replied and turned to his two companions. "Miyuki, Minami, let's go."

The two girls nodded and followed Tatsuya's lead toward the large sedan parked in front of the house.

Today was the big move. They were leaving the home under the name of Tatsuya and Miyuki's father, and Miyuki was headed to the Yotsuba family's Tokyo headquarters in Chofu for her personal security. All her necessary belongings, including clothing, small items, and a compact study terminal, had already been moved. The data from their underground research lab had also been completely transferred to the underground research facility in the Tokyo headquarters building. And this wasn't a mere copy of the data; it was a full transfer. Their current private research lab was scheduled for complete demolition in a few days.

Miyuki sat in the back seat of the sedan, followed by Tatsuya. Minami joined them in the front passenger seat. While this wasn't a limousine, the seats were very spacious. Even Tatsuya, who was seated behind the driver's seat, experienced no type of discomfort. Once everyone was buckled up, Hyougo sat behind the wheel and smoothly began the journey from Fuchu to Chofu. For such a short distance, the travel time was almost the same as using a family car or a cabinet. Especially considering the time it took to walk to the station, driving was the fastest mode of transportation.

Hyougo was a very good driver. The car itself probably had something to do with it, but the ride was smooth with minimal jolting. Neither Tatsuya nor Miyuki said a word during the short yet comfortable drive, and Minami was as quiet as always. Reading their cues, Hyougo also refrained from initiating any form of conversation.

He parked the car in the underground garage of the Chofu building. It was a typical parking lot with white lines and an embedded automatic parking guide transmitter. Toward the back of the garage, there was a space equipped with an automatic inspection device.

"This way," Hyougo said, leading the way into an elevator that provided direct access to Miyuki's residence. Only Tatsuya and Miyuki could use it without a key.

"In the case of an emergency, you can use this elevator to descend to other floors," Hyougo explained with a modest smile. "But you can only board it from the first floor, basement, rooftop, and in front of your room. The rooftop, by the way, is where the heliport we used the other day is located."

He guided the group to a room that was luxurious no matter how you looked at it, but only in the most refined way. Miyuki immediately fell in love with it.

"Will you be staying here tonight, Master Tatsuya?" Hyougo asked.

It would have been strange for Hyougo to ask Tatsuya if he would be staying at his own home, but there was a good reason behind this. Miyuki would be living in this residence with Minami serving as her maid and guardian. Tatsuya, however, was set to move to a villa in Izu as per Maya's instructions. The Chofu building was not yet Tatsuya's home. When Miyuki had said she was sad about moving, it had been less about leaving their familiar house behind and more related to being separated from Tatsuya for a while.

"No, I won't be staying," Tatsuya replied. "We can leave as soon as the villa is ready."

"Understood," Hyougo said with a nod. "Then please feel free to relax for a couple more hours."

He gave the couple a sweeping bow and left the room.

Miyuki led Tatsuya to the living room sofa, and they both took a seat. The villa in Izu was actually already prepared, but Hyougo had taken a hint and given the two some extra time together. Tatsuya and Miyuki recognized his kindness deep down.

Tatsuya traveled to Izu in the compact VTOL he had taken once before. The flight lasted about thirty minutes. This was longer than expected, but it was because the skies were so congested on this day. It had only been a matter of time before airborne traffic jams became a reality.

As Tatsuya expected, the villa lay deep in the mountains, away from the former antiaircraft site now converted into a golf course. The location provided the perfect quiet environment, free from any disturbances.

"Did my mother—I mean, stepmother—really undergo treatment out here in the middle of nowhere?" Tatsuya couldn't help but voice this sudden question. He quickly corrected himself to refer to Miya as his stepmother, since Maya was officially his biological mother now.

"I was told Ms. Miya needed a quiet environment to heal," Hyougo responded.

Tatsuya immediately understood the vagueness of his response. Psion noise generated by crowds had always been a burden for Miya. Tatsuya realized once again how much of an effort his mother had made for her children's sake. But whether it had been for his sake or Miyuki's, he would never know.

Hyougo guided Tatsuya into the villa as soon as they arrived. The interior was arranged in a way that helped facilitate a smooth daily routine. The research facilities were even more comprehensive than in his Fuchu residence.

"Please give me a call if you need anything and it will be delivered right away," Hyougo said. "I have also left the Freed Suit and *Wingless* here, so you are welcome to use them anytime."

The Freed Suit was a flight-combat ensemble disguised as a regular riding suit, and *Wingless* was an armored bike linked to the Freed Suit. These tools would prove useful in the event of an armed attack, but also when he needed to make a quick trip to Tokyo.

"Thank you," Tatsuya said.

"No problem at all," Hyougo replied with a smile. "I wish you the best here."

"Thanks, and fly safely."

"I will. Until we meet again."

Hyougo left the villa and boarded the VTOL. Tatsuya could hear the vehicle's propellers spin away as he stood alone in his new home.

Five hundred kilometers west of Newfoundland, the large USNA aircraft carrier Enterprise was anchored in the Atlantic's open waters. It was a colossal vessel with a length of about six hundred meters. Despite its size approaching twice that of prewar nuclear-powered aircraft carriers, the vessel was famous for not using nuclear reactors at all. When the International Magic Association had conducted external inspections while the carrier had been underway, preliminary findings had indicated the Enterprise was nuclear-free. Given its founding history, the International Magic Association was equipped with technology that could detect nuclear fission reactions with absolute reliability. So it was telling that they had not been able to find any traces of nuclear power usage aboard the enormous vessel.

Further investigation would require access to the interior of the ship, but the USNA did not allow this for operational military vessels. Consequently, the Enterprise's power source remained a mystery to this day.

A small rotary aircraft escorted by four fighter jets attempted to land on the Enterprise. It appeared to be a high-speed craft without the vertical takeoff and landing capabilities of VTOLs or STOVLs.

That aircraft is carrying Bezobrazov, Lina thought as she looked up at the approaching craft with her golden eyes. She was in her Stars uniform and briefly removed her mask.

Igor Andreivich Bezobrazov, a member of the Thirteen Apostles and citizen of the New Soviet Union, was well-versed in the strategic magic spell Tuman Bomba and known by the alias *Igniter* in the United States. Until his recent appearance on a televised interview, he had been classified a New Soviet Union military secret that only the USNA military had been privy to. While the USNA was prohibited from constantly monitoring Bezobrazov's whereabouts, they did have some information about him. The strategic magician was also a member of the New Soviet Academy and considered the foremost authority on modern magic in his country. This made obfuscating his appearance and location an inherent challenge.

The true nature of Bezobrazov's strategic magic spell Tuman Bomba—both how it worked and its effects—was something no one knew. The only thing the USNA was aware of was the spell's name and its ability to cause explosive damage over an expansive area. It was also clear it had led to the previous Sirius's death in a military conflict between the USNA and New Soviet Union across the Bering Strait eight years ago.

To a member of the Stars like Lina, Bezobrazov was someone she must surpass if she was to claim the title of the world's strongest magician. However, that opportunity may never arrive if he decided to join the Dione Project.

As a small VTOL approached the Enterprise, it was clear the aircraft carrier's landing procedure hadn't advanced since one hundred and fifty years ago. Aircraft without vertical landing capabilities utilized an angled deck and a series of arresting cables and hooks to forcibly lower their speed. Even with its catapult extended to eight hundred meters, the Enterprise could not reliably stop the aircraft with thrust brakes alone. Launching technology may have progressed significantly, but landing technology had not moved beyond the use of deceleration cables.

Lina felt a strong sense of unease as the VTOL aircraft approached the Enterprise.

Have the arresting hooks not been deployed? she thought in disbelief.

Just as she realized this, a commotion spread across the deck.

"The engine's output is too restricted!" an Enterprise staff member exclaimed.

"At this rate, it's going to crash!" another voice yelled.

In order to prevent the worst, Lina quickly manipulated her CAD. Suddenly, the VTOL aircraft was enveloped in psion light. But Lina had not yet initiated any magic.

Is the light coming from inside the aircraft?! she thought.

Lina sensed the magic around the VTOL coming from within it. Just then, the aircraft's landing gear caught on the deck and the vehicle smoothly reduced its speed as usual.

It used a combination of inertial and acceleration control to decelerate so naturally, Lina thought in awe.

Normally, a landing required thousands of meters of runway, but the VTOL had managed to land in one hundred meters without any sign of difficulty.

How did they achieve such precise control? Lina wondered.

Despite the Enterprise's enormous size, it still experienced some motion due to the wind. Lina doubted she could have ever achieved such elegant deceleration.

So this is Bezobrazov the Igniter's true power, she thought, with absolute confidence he had been the one behind the display of magic.

A transport aircraft carrying MacLeod landed on the Enterprise shortly after Bezobrazov's arrival, and the meeting began.

The attendees included Edward Clark, Igor Andreivich Bezobrazov, William MacLeod, and Lina in her Angie Sirius disguise. Lina stood behind Clark, who was the only non-magician in the room. Both Bezobrazov and MacLeod were strategic magicians. Angie Sirius was in attendance at MacLeod's suggestion that Clark should have a strategic magician accompanying him for protection. The meeting commenced with Bezobrazov's sudden appeal to Clark.

"Dr. Clark, we made a promise," he said. "You must tell me the identity of the strategic magician Taurus Silver."

Lina's heart leaped in her chest. Since she now had her helmet off, the three men in the room were quick to notice her surprise. Bezobrazov seemed taken aback by Angie's reaction, and it appeared to dampen his persistence. But this didn't significantly change the direction of the conversation.

"Don't tell us you would dare keep information from your own allies," MacLeod said with a sigh.

"I only recently discovered his identity myself," Clark said, blatantly lying through his teeth before continuing. "Taurus Silver's real name is Tatsuya Shiba, and he is one of the direct heirs to Japan's Yotsuba clan."

After putting together a rough plan for future actions, the meeting concluded without any significant conflicts. Once it was over, Lina's mission was also complete. Left without anything to do until her return flight, she wandered through the Enterprise with the captain's permission. While officially touring the premises, her thoughts were captivated by someone who wasn't even physically present.

So Tatsuya is the strategic magician behind Scorching Halloween, she thought.

After Taurus Silver's identity had been revealed, she couldn't remember anything Clark, Bezobrazov, and MacLeod had discussed. It wasn't that she had forgotten; she had simply stopped listening. Only fragments of the conversation lingered in her mind. Ultimately, Taurus Silver's identity came as such a shock that she hadn't been able to keep up with the three men's discussion.

Two Octobers prior, a strategic magic spell known as Material Burst had scorched the southern tip of the Korean Peninsula. Its caster was Tatsuya Shiba. The true identity of Taurus Silver—the genius magic engineer who had successfully developed flight magic for practical use—was also Tatsuya Shiba.

Of course! Lina exclaimed inwardly. *I had a feeling this was the case from the very beginning.*

Last January, Lina had infiltrated Japan to uncover the identity of the strategic magician behind Scorching Halloween. All she had known at the time was that the USNA called him the Great Bomber and that her mission was to address the threat he posed on the global stage. Military intelligence had ordered her to investigate Tatsuya in particular, who was identified as a suspect. Now their intuition proved to be correct.

But Tatsuya never showed any signs, Lina reasoned. *He has a different kind of magic...*

She paused for a moment, another part of her mind calmly countering her own thoughts.

Of course he didn't show any signs. He is skilled enough to hide it.

And of course he had a different kind of magic. He wouldn't reveal his strategic magic to just anyone.

Suddenly, her thoughts intensified.

You didn't even know he was the direct Yotsuba heir.

He tricked you.

"That's right. Tatsuya tricked me," she whispered to herself.

Yet strangely, she didn't feel angry at all. Everything seemed to suddenly make sense—the sympathy she felt for Tatsuya and the mercy he had granted her. Both most likely stemmed from a mutual sense of empathy toward those trapped by fate to be military weapons.

Lina shook her head, attempting to banish the endless spiral of negative thoughts from her mind. Suddenly, she was thrust back into reality.

"Uh-oh…" she gasped.

This is a restricted area! she realized, reprimanding herself for day-dreaming. Then she turned her frustrations to the safety staff for not having stopped her from entering. Regardless of who was at fault, she had to get out of here.

As commander of the Stars, Lina had the authority to access most classified information. However, having authority and exercising it were two different things. Information was classified for a reason, and delving into secrets she shouldn't know was asking for trouble. That was why Lina urgently sought a way out.

But suddenly, she forgot her rush, her face twisting into a frown.

Wait, she thought. *What are these psionic waves I'm sensing?*

The psionic waves only became apparent when she entered the restricted area. There must have been a grid of Reaction Stones embedded in the partition separating this space from the rest of the ship to conceal the psions' presence. For a moment, Lina thought this might be a measure to conceal a nuclear reactor, but she quickly changed her mind.

Reaction Stones converted psionic waves into electrical signals. As a secondary effect, the stones dampened the psions' presence, making them essentially undetectable. What the stones couldn't do, however, was absorb or block radiation.

Is this some sort of magic, then? Lina thought. *But why...?*

With the suspicion of forbidden nuclear power dispelled, she began to wonder what else the power she sensed could be. Magic was an individual type of power. Usually, multiple magicians cooperating to cast a single spell was rare, while not completely unheard of. Even in such rare cases where magicians did cooperate, they only did so in groups of two or three at the most. However, the psionic waves Lina sensed indicated there were at least ten, even twenty magicians being forced to contribute to a single spell.

What's going on here? she wondered. *Forcing magic out of magicians is prohibited by military regulations.*

She recalled a Prionace developer telling her about experiments during World War III where multiple magicians had been forcibly linked to execute large-scale spells. It had been a joint experiment program between the USNA and Japan—which had been a closer ally at the time than it was now. But the results had ultimately been deemed a failure and the experiment had been put to rest.

The main cause behind the failure had been the collapse of the magicians' egos. Participating magicians had lost their ability to think on their own and ultimately could no longer keep themselves alive. The Prionace developer had said the forced mental link was the culprit. As a result, tampering with collective magic had become strictly forbidden.

Yet Lina sensed a group of magicians was being compelled to read an activation sequence and forcibly activate a spell in this very area. Technology that completely turned magicians into mere components of magic machinery, ignoring their free will, explicitly violated the rules of human rights imposed by the USNA military.

The spell itself is simple; it's just spinning a flywheel, Lina thought. *But performing a simple task for an extended period inevitably causes stress. They clearly need so many magicians because of the wheel's large mass and high rotation speed.*

Suddenly, she shouted out loud: "There's no way!"

A power-generation system? Is this the secret behind the Enterprise's energy force?

Lina clamped her hands over her mouth so as not to make any more noise and checked her surroundings. There wasn't a single soul in sight. She noticed some surveillance cameras, but it probably looked as if she had walked into the restricted area by mistake and was flailing around. At least, that was what she convinced herself of as she scurried back the way she had come.

Lina shared an aircraft with Clark on her trip back to headquarters. While her escort mission was already complete, arranging a separate flight back to the mainland was considered an unnecessary use of resources. This gave Lina no choice but to accompany Clark back to Washington D.C.

"Thank you for your service today, Major Sirius," he greeted.

"Not a problem," Lina answered a little coldly. She didn't want to speak to anyone right now. In fact, she wanted nothing more than to get out of her "clown suit" and fall into a dreamless sleep. It took all her strength to keep the frustration out of her voice. Perhaps it was Clark's young age, but he paid no mind to Lina's behavior.

"I probably don't need to tell you this, but please keep Taurus Silver's identity to yourself," he continued. "Colonel Walker and Colonel Balance do not know about it."

"I have a duty to report back to my superiors," Lina said freely.

"That's all right," Clark reassured her. "I promise you won't face any consequences for omitting a few details."

He was not military personnel. In fact, he was merely an NSA technician. He didn't have the authority to intervene in military rewards or punishments. Just before Lina could mention this, Clark spoke first.

"If you reveal Taurus Silver's true identity," he warned, "he might decide to expose your identity as well."

Lina was speechless for a moment.

"How do you know about that?" she gasped.

"Allowing you to make contact with Silver at all was a failure on the part of the military," Clark asserted. "You're still young; it's understandable you might let your emotions get the better of you."

Lina was shocked. Clark was insinuating he knew more about her activities in Japan than the military did.

"Oh, that's right," he added furtively. "I'd appreciate it if you avoided reporting about the truth of the Enterprise as well."

With that, he effectively sealed Lina's lips.

[6]

From Monday onward, Tatsuya didn't show up at First High. While his actions on the surface appeared to be nothing more than an individual student's decision, they sent ripples that went beyond the school.

Somewhere in Tokyo, members responsible for the covert actions of the National Defense Force's Intelligence Department gathered in a top secret conference room.

"It seems the high school boy has begun living alone," one member mentioned.

"This is the perfect opportunity," another ventured. "Unlike when he was living in the city, we won't have to worry about civilians now."

"Wait." A cautionary voice rose from the table.

"What's the problem, Inukai?"

The cautionary voice belonged to none other than Chief Inukai, Tsukasa Tooyama's direct superior, who understood the dangers Tatsuya posed.

"The fact that we can deploy sufficient forces on our end means Tatsuya doesn't need to hold back, either. It is far too dangerous to attack recklessly now," he explained.

"Are you saying it's a trap?" a voice asked.

"Not exactly," Inukai said, "but it's important to remember our target is a member of the Yotsuba clan, which is often called untouchable. It would be unwise to attack unprepared."

"I agree," Onda said with a nod. "You all saw what happened at Nansou Detention Camp despite our ample defensive forces. While the roles of offense and defense may be flipped, it would be best to avoid dealing with the boy on our own."

"Onda, do you know of any allies who could help us?" Inukai asked.

"He is not exactly an ally," Onda said, "but I do have one person in mind who we could use."

"Please tell us more," Inukai insisted.

"It appears the head of the Juumonji clan will be visiting Tatsuya Shiba's hermit abode in Izu in the near future as a representative of the Magic Association," Onda reported duly to Inukai alone before turning to the entire table. "I cannot say what they will talk about, but it surely has to do with the USNA project."

He was lying about one thing. He knew Tatsuya was Taurus Silver and that Katsuto was going to try to convince him to join the project. But he kept this to himself.

"I believe the Magic Association supports the project and is attempting to convince the Yotsuba clan to join its development ranks," a senior section chief offered.

Other than Onda, none of the adults at the table had yet connected Tatsuya to Taurus Silver. They thought highly of the high schooler's battle skills because they had experienced them firsthand. But they had no knowledge of Tatsuya's abilities or technical expertise. This was why they failed to connect the high school student with the top-tier magic engineer.

"I see. That poses quite the opportunity for us," the deputy director, who held the highest position at this table, said, nodding subtly but decisively. "The Yotsuba clan's uncooperative attitude was already evident at that earlier meeting."

He was referring to the Ten Master Clans' Youth Council held in April. Although this meeting was unrelated to the current situation, it was loosely connected at the surface level.

"Any negotiations between Tatsuya Shiba and the head of the Juumonji clan are likely to fail. But if the two were to engage in combat, Katsuto Juumonji would win. Isn't that right, Inukai?" the deputy director continued.

"Yes, sir," Inukai agreed with confidence. "Sergeant Major Tooyama, or rather, the Tooyama clan believed that to be true."

The Tooyama clan had never taken a seat among the Twenty-Eight Families, let alone been considered a candidate for one of the Ten Master Clans. However, in terms of military magic, they were on par with both the Yotsuba and Juumonji clans. The National Defense Force's Intelligence Department was convinced of this. Military magicians excelled in combat, analytical, and tactical assessments. The Tooyama clan was the only Number among the Twenty-Eight Families to receive military training from birth.

"I doubt the head of the Juumonji clan will kill Tatsuya," Inukai continued, "but once he defeats the younger boy in battle, Tatsuya's defenses should be lowered."

"It's also helpful that the Juumonji clan does not oppose the National Defense Force in any way," the deputy director mentioned.

"True." Inukai nodded.

"Let's act as soon as the Juumonji clan does and have Sergeant Major Tooyama deployed for good measure," the deputy director proposed. "This time, our goal is not simply to deal with Tatsuya Shiba, but to crush the Yotsuba clan's security."

"U-understood," Inukai replied, this time with a hint of hesitation in his voice.

"Don't worry, Inukai," the deputy director said. "The Yotsuba clan has faith in Tatsuya's fighting abilities. I doubt they will give him any additional protection. Most of their energy will surely be focused on Tatsuya's fiancée."

He turned to Onda.

"That's correct," Onda said with a respectful nod.

"Hello, every— Hmm?" Shiina looked puzzled as she entered the student council office.

"What's wrong, Shiina?" Izumi asked, turning in her chair to face the freshman.

"Oh, um...I was just wondering where Pixie was," she replied.

Sure enough, Pixie was no longer in her usual corner.

"She belongs to Tatsuya," Minami responded.

She pulled a cleaning cloth from a box containing a portable vacuum and a set of cleaning tools and began wiping the tables. Shiina didn't dare offer to help. After knowing each other for a month, she knew Minami wouldn't easily delegate such a task to a younger student.

The older girl continued, "I sent her with Tatsuya so she could care for him."

Shiina had only heard half of what she'd said when Miyuki walked into the office.

"Hi, Miyuki!" Izumi greeted, as hyper as ever.

"Hello," Shiina greeted the student council president placidly before turning back to Minami. "So does that mean—"

Before she could finish her sentence, someone poked her from behind.

"Eek!" she yelped, jumping into the air.

She spun around to find Shizuku shaking her head.

"Ki-Kitayama, what was that about?" Shiina whimpered.

"Shiina," Honoka whispered, "it's probably best if we don't talk about Tatsuya."

The freshman girl quickly shut her mouth. She knew when to take a hint.

* * *

The day after she was separated from Tatsuya, Miyuki attended classes and completed her student council duties as usual. To classmates who didn't normally interact with Tatsuya, Miyuki probably seemed the same as always. Even friends who walked home with her for the first time in a while may not have noticed any difference. The ability to sense something was off was a testament to their bonds of friendship.

Erika, for example, didn't share a classroom with Miyuki and wasn't involved in any official school activities. The two girls' time together was much shorter than her regular classmates'. Still, she was able to detect something was amiss thanks to her sharp observational skills.

"Hey, Miyuki, are you okay?" Erika asked.

"Yes, I'm fine," Miyuki replied. "Thank you for asking."

She understood empathy was a mark of true friendship, so she made sure to never be dismissive or cold. Moreover, Miyuki didn't feel embarrassed admitting she missed Tatsuya when he wasn't around. For her, this was just a natural part of life. She existed for Tatsuya and his presence was indispensable to her. Her friends, of course, knew this, so there was no need to hide her feelings at this point.

"If you don't mind me asking," Honoka said cautiously, "where is Tatsuya now?"

"I don't mind," Miyuki reassured her. "He is currently taking a break at a family villa in Izu. I am glad he is getting some rest for once."

"Izu? I'd say I envied him if I didn't know about the mess he's in," Erika said, half jokingly and half serious.

"That 'mess he's in' is exactly why he had to run off to Izu," Leo countered.

"Shut it, Leo. I knew that much," Erika snapped back. "That annoying streak of yours makes it impossible for anyone to like you."

"Hey, that's a low blow!" Leo said with a miffed expression. "I may not be as popular as Tatsuya, but I'm not completely hopeless with the ladies. Right, Sakurai?"

The typical group of seniors joined by juniors Kasumi, Izumi, and Minami, and freshmen Shiina and Saburou, were all gathered around a table at the usual coffee shop. Leo felt comfortable speaking to Minami because they were both in the mountaineering club. Although Minami couldn't participate much due to her involvement in the student council, she occasionally acted like the club's manager by offering rice balls made by the cooking club.

"…Right," she replied, somewhat reluctantly.

"Geez," Erika cringed, "I hope I don't end up flaunting my power like you do."

"What'd you say?!" Leo growled.

Erika ignored him and turned to Minami. "You know you don't have to defend him, even though he's the club president, right?"

"Uh…" Minami glanced apprehensively between Erika and Leo.

"Erika, Leo, please leave Minami alone," Miyuki implored.

The two exchanged glances before compliantly nodding their heads. Thanks to Miyuki, Minami was finally able to escape the line of fire. Just then, Mizuki changed the subject.

"Will Tatsuya be returning to Tokyo this weekend?" she asked.

As an awkwardness enveloped the group, Miyuki sadly shook her head.

"I don't think he will be back here for a while," she said. "Too many troublesome people to bother him."

"D-do you think we could visit him?" Honoka ventured bravely.

Miyuki thought for a moment. "That is a very good question."

"He might be getting some disruptive guests, after all," Honoka added.

"You think so?" Kasumi asked.

"It's definitely a possibility," Izumi mused.

Miyuki gave the twins an affectionate smile. "Even if that did happen and those visitors were part of your family, you cannot get in your father and brother's way."

"But Miyuki," Izumi gushed, "we'll always be on your side!"

Yet Kasumi was visibly unnerved.

"Izumi," Miyuki chided, "saying things like that will only make your sister uncomfortable."

"You're always on my side, right, Kasumi?" Izumi asked.

"Well, yes, but…" Kasumi began, looking even more uneasy.

"Izumi," Miyuki interrupted with a wry smile, "just promise me you won't do anything rash. Tatsuya and I really do want to avoid any conflict with your father."

"All right," Izumi conceded. She had a weakness born out of love. When Miyuki made an earnest request, it was impossible for Izumi to resist.

"Then you have to promise us you won't put up a brave front with us," Erika insisted with a smile.

"I just don't want you to do anything rash," Miyuki said.

"We won't," Erika reassured shamelessly. "As long as we can help it."

Her expression was so nonchalant that Miyuki could only muster a vague smile in response.

The Magic University didn't have any hobby clubs, but it did host various club activities. Prominent sports clubs, for example, were well-equipped and came with personal trainers. Many magic career paths required physical fitness and agility, so these clubs supplemented the lack of practical physical education within the university's curriculum. Of course, not all students joined clubs, since it wasn't mandatory. While Katsuto had served as the head of the club association in high school, he had decided not to join a club when he had entered university.

He had responsibilities as the head of the Juumonji clan, so he made it a point to return home as early as possible. It was rare for him to leave as late as he did on this day, but it had taken him longer than expected to complete his practical training report. With all the work he would have to catch up on due to the unplanned delay on his mind, Katsuto hurried toward the station. As he passed through the school gate, a voice called out to him from behind.

"Juumonji!"

Katsuto recognized the voice without turning around. Its owner was someone who didn't mince words and often ended up causing more disruptions than expected. Yet for some reason, despite his pressing family duties, he couldn't help but stop in his tracks.

"Juumonji!" the voice repeated.

"I heard you already, Saegusa," Katsuto sighed. "You don't need to yell so loud."

Mayumi, who had been rushing to Katsuto's side, quickly came to a stop and gave him an awkward smile. She didn't quite give him a typical ditzy expression, but her gestures gave off a playful demeanor.

"I'm sorry for bothering you," she apologized.

"It's fine. What do you need?" Katsuto said impatiently.

His bluntness didn't mean he refused to give Mayumi the time of day. He simply felt comfortable enough around her to completely be himself.

"I have something I wanted to ask you," Mayumi explained. "Mind if I join you in a cabinet?"

"It will make your commute longer," Katsuto said.

"Only by about twenty minutes, tops," Mayumi said with a shrug. "I don't mind."

Contemporary short-distance public transportation systems, like cabinets, usually provided direct service to disembarking stations rather than dropping off passengers along the way to individual destinations. On the other hand, it wasn't entirely impossible for multiple passengers to share a ride. This, however, involved an element of luck. If there were no waiting passengers at the station where one rider needed to disembark, the cabinet could continue to the next station with the remaining passengers onboard. Even if there were other people at the first station, the other passenger could simply wait in line for the next vehicle.

Cabinets ensured privacy within their compartments. The likelihood of conversations inside the vehicle being overheard was extremely low. Therefore, it was fairly common for businessmen or couples to utilize cabinets for confidential discussions.

Mayumi's invitation to share a ride was precisely for this purpose. Katsuto made sure the cabinet's initial destination was the nearest station to the Saegusa family residence.

"You're such a gentleman," Mayumi giggled.

"It's just a common courtesy," Katsuto replied, unfazed. "So what did you want to ask me?"

Mayumi's smile instantly vanished. "I heard you're going to visit Tatsuya."

"Did your father tell you that?" Katsuto asked.

"Yes, but he didn't say why you're going," Mayumi replied.

Katsuto leaned back in his seat, folded his arms, and closed his eyes.

"I can't tell you that," he said.

"Thanks. I think I got it now," she said.

Katsuto opened his eyes to find Mayumi winking at him.

"The only hint I had to go off of was that you were visiting a Japanese high school student, even though that and the fact it was being kept such a tight secret pretty much gave it away," Mayumi explained discreetly. "It looks like my hunch was right."

Katsuto remained silent until she called his name again.

"Juumonji?"

"What?" he sighed.

Mayumi clearly wanted something from him.

"Could you take me with you?" she pleaded.

This request took Katsuto off guard for a moment, but he quickly regained his composure.

"Why?" he asked.

"I doubt you'll be able to convince Tatsuya peacefully," she explained.

"You're probably right," he said.

"I also doubt you'll leave without the answer you want."

"……"

"Don't get me wrong," Mayumi said. "That doesn't mean I think Tatsuya will beat you. He's strong, but you're definitely stronger."

"But?" Katsuto said, anticipating her next statement.

"*But*," she added predictably, "I don't think Tatsuya will go down easily. In fact, with his healing magic, he might fight to the death."

"Is his healing magic really that powerful?" Katsuto asked, unfolding his arms and leaning forward in his seat.

"Yes," Mayumi nodded, looking him straight in the eye. "It's technically not even healing magic. But anyway, I think you should take me with you so you can avoid unnecessary conflict."

"You want to help me convince Shiba to join the project?" Katsuto asked.

"I promise I won't get in your way," she insisted.

Katsuto dropped his gaze and sighed.

"It was just meant to be a conversation in the first place, but you're probably right," he relented. "Bringing you along with me would ensure a peaceful resolution. You know Shiba better than I do anyway."

"I don't know about that last part," Mayumi said skeptically. "When were you planning to go?"

"This Sunday, if Shiba is free," Katsuto said. "I'm going to take the car, so I'll pick you up."

"Wow, how kind of you," Mayumi said with a smile.

The two were quiet for the rest of the ride, but it was anything but awkward.

◇ ◇ ◇

The day after her escort mission on the aircraft carrier Enterprise, Lina unenthusiastically attended training. On the way back to their quarters, the Stars's number two, Benjamin Canopus, expressed genuine concern.

"You seem off today, commander," he noted. "Are you feeling okay?"

"It's nothing to worry about, Ben," Lina replied. "Sorry for being so sloppy today."

"No need to apologize," he said, shaking his head. "It's only natural for humans to have ups and downs. But are you sure you're okay?"

"Yes," Lina assured. "I must have just been more nervous than I thought in the presence of two Apostles yesterday."

"Well, it *was* a diplomatic meeting," Canopus said, nodding with understanding. "Anyone would feel exhausted under all that pressure not to make mistakes in the face of foreign guests."

"Are you saying I'm clumsy?" Lina asked.

"Oh, no, not at all," he said, quickly averting his gaze.

Lina felt an angry twitch at her temple.

"Anyway," Canopus continued, "the best thing to do at a time like this is rest. Take care, commander."

He flashed her a cheerful smile and walked away. Lina glared after him until she realized she couldn't stay in the same spot forever. She relaxed her shoulders and turned toward her room.

Lina felt a bit better now that Canopus had annoyed her, but it wasn't enough to remove the lingering knot in her chest. Even after a shower, she still didn't feel refreshed. She knew what was causing her to feel this way—the conditions of the magicians she had seen, or rather felt, on the Enterprise.

Lina had never felt much discomfort or aversion to the idea of magicians being treated as weapons. Her strongest doubts had arisen when she had been in Japan interacting with Tatsuya.

She sat in front of her mirror, wearing only a bath towel and hardly aware of what she was doing. Her thoughts had completely taken over her mind.

Tatsuya didn't deny the fact that magicians fight, she thought.

Tatsuya didn't deny the fact that magicians became soldiers.

Tatsuya didn't explicitly deny the fact that magicians become weapons.

Tatsuya did deny the fact that I should continue my military career.

Come to think of it, Lina vaguely remembered hearing something about Tatsuya's goal—a world where magicians didn't have to become weapons. Maybe she was misremembering and Tatsuya had never said anything like that. But one thing felt certain: Tatsuya was trying to create a society where magicians would not be forced to be living artillery.

Upon returning home and being away from Tatsuya, Lina had stopped grappling with such thoughts. She had believed once again that it was natural for magicians who enlisted in the military to use magic as a form of combat. The idea of a world where magicians were no longer forced to be weapons had felt like a fleeting delusion.

Lina had joined the military of her own volition. Magicians, too, assumed the role of weapons by their own free will. No matter how it might seem from an outsider's perspective, magicians had freedom of choice.

That's what I've always believed, Lina thought. *Or at least forced myself to believe. But the Enterprise's system is the perfect example of what Tatsuya talked about.*

"I should warn him," she murmured to herself.

As she reached for the phone, her hand froze in midair.

Wait. What am I doing? she thought incredulously. *What would I even warn Tatsuya about? The fact that Bezobrazov and MacLeod are after him?*

Though she had just showered, a subtle yet unpleasant sweat began to bead on her forehead, and an eerie chill ran down her spine.

"Ha-ha… Ha-ha-ha-ha…"

Laughter escaped her lips half-consciously.

"What in the world am I doing?" she said aloud.

If she stopped laughing, she felt she might trigger a panic attack. Remembering what Tatsuya had told her was not the worst thing she could do. Considering leaking military information to warn him with her undoubtedly monitored personal phone, however, was absolutely ridiculous.

Am I really in that much shock? Lina pondered.

She thought she had come to terms with the fact that magicians were being used as cogs, as fuel in a system. She thought she had accepted the fact that military personnel's free will was restricted.

"Is that why Tatsuya said that to me?" she whispered.

Their late-night conversation echoed once more in her ears.

"Lina, if you ever want to leave the Stars… If you ever want to quit being a soldier…"

Did he know I wasn't cut out for the military? Lina wondered.

By now, she had lost all awareness of her own thoughts. She stood up, wiped the sweat off her face, and headed back into the shower to warm up her body. Lina untied her bath towel and let the hot water hit her skin. All of a sudden, she could no longer recall the thoughts that had spiraled around in her head in front of the bathroom mirror.

[7]

Katsuto's e-mail reached Tatsuya on Wednesday evening. It asked about Tatsuya's availability on Sunday. The most intriguing part was that the e-mail had been forwarded from the Yotsuba main house. This meant Katsuto's meeting was not centered around the hierarchical dynamic the two boys had had at First High; it was a proposition from one Ten Master Clan to another.

"Do you have somewhere you need to be, Tatsuya?"

Fumiya Kuroba, who had just arrived at the Izu villa a few minutes earlier, spoke to Tatsuya as the older boy returned to the sofa. At about the same time, Pixie arrived, carrying two cups of coffee. Ignoring the robot's presence, Tatsuya responded to Fumiya's question.

"No, the head of the Juumonji clan just asked me if he can come over on Sunday in an e-mail relayed through the main house. Do you know about this?"

"Not really," Fumiya replied.

Tatsuya reached for his coffee cup and urged Fumiya to do the same before it got cold. Fumiya extended one hand, sparkling with freshly manicured nails, toward the table, while the other swept through the bobbed hair framing his cheeks. Then he lightly pressed his reddened lips to his cup.

"Interesting," Tatsuya murmured. "By the way, it's rare to see you without your sister."

"Ayako wanted to see you, too, but I was asked to come alone," Fumiya replied, setting his coffee cup back on the table.

As he leaned toward the table, he unconsciously adjusted the slightly disheveled hem of his skirt.

"So tell me what exact orders bring you here," Tatsuya prompted with a curious tone. "I assume your outfit is part of the instructions you were given."

This last comment made the younger boy blush. Fumiya's dress was much more elegant than anything your average high school girl would wear.

"Well, you see, people can easily recognize me on the street," Fumiya replied.

"Oh, I see," Tatsuya said with a nod. "It's dangerous for you to come in contact with me right now without a disguise."

This made sense to Tatsuya. Fumiya had gained some recognition during the previous year's Nine School Competition. While it was already something of an open secret that he belonged to the Yotsuba family, the main house still had no intention of publicly acknowledging his existence. This was a rather unfortunate situation for Fumiya, since he had no personal interest in cross-dressing.

"So what brings you here?" Tatsuya asked again.

Fumiya sat up in his seat. "This villa might soon be under attack."

"By the National Defense Force?" Tatsuya asked, unsurprised.

"Yes," Fumiya answered, though not nearly as calmly. His adorably made-up face twitched anxiously.

"Calm down," Tatsuya said. "You're just the messenger."

This made Fumiya feel a little braver.

"The Yotsuba family said they won't send backup," he reported, clenching his skirt in both fists. At this point, he was prepared for the worst.

But Tatsuya merely replied, "Of course not."

"Huh?" Fumiya gasped, confused.

"This is nothing like an internal conflict among the Ten Master Clans," Tatsuya explained. "At this time, facing off with the National Defense Force isn't a wise move. There's no reason an entire clan should be forced to go underground for the sake of one person. It would only lead to steep losses."

"And you're okay with that?" Fumiya asked.

"What are you so nervous about?" Tatsuya asked back.

Fumiya suddenly realized the trembling in his arms wasn't due to excitement or tension. Fear had taken hold of him.

"All I have to do is take them all down myself," Tatsuya said casually, as if stating a basic mathematical formula.

Fumiya's eyes widened, his lips parting slightly. Though he would hate to hear this, his white teeth and pink tongue, peeking through the gap between his rouge lips, were enticing enough to make someone want to kiss him. For a brief moment, Tatsuya cast a glance of pity toward his second cousin and his ability to exude such an indescribable girlish charm. But Tatsuya's steely expression soon returned.

"Luckily, I have a suit and motorcycle here," he reassured.

The suit he described wasn't your average riding suit. Fumiya was aware the Yotsuba family had moved the self-developed powered armor suit and motorcycle to this villa.

"I even have Torus, Trident, and Lancehead with me," Tatsuya added. "The secluded mountains and woodlands are now my playground. Unless I'm dealing with enemies at the level of Imakashin and the Great Tengu, I don't intend to fall behind."

Torus was short for *Silver Torus*, a fully thought-operated CAD in bracelet form; Trident was short for *Silver Horn Custom Trident*, Tatsuya's favorite gun-type CAD system; and Lancehead was a CAD attachment specifically designed for the Baryon Lance. With this level of equipment, Tatsuya would surely win any battle. Unless, as he said, he was facing enemies at the level of Imakashin (Yakumo

Kokonoe) and the Great Tengu (Harunobu Kazama), it didn't matter if his opponents numbered in the dozens or hundreds. Suddenly, Fumiya noticed his trembling had stopped.

Fumiya had arrived at the villa in a taxi that was parked outside. Typically, the fare would be exorbitant if he had kept it waiting for so long. But Tatsuya knew better. He surmised the taxi had been reserved upon realizing the driver was in the Kuroba family's traditional black attire. Fumiya put on a wide-brimmed hat he had arrived in, and Tatsuya walked him to the entrance.

"I've deleted the surveillance data, but be careful on your way back," Tatsuya said.

"I appreciate it," Fumiya replied with a grateful bow that matched his fancy dress to a T.

The surveillance data Tatsuya had mentioned referred to the images captured by hidden surveillance cameras, probably belonging to the military's Intelligence Department. Deleting this data would make it impossible to identify Fumiya, especially in a dress. Fumiya's disguise was meant to deceive the naked eye, but it was his wide-brimmed hat that helped him avoid detection via spy satellites or stratospheric platform cameras.

"About that e-mail I mentioned earlier... I assume my mother is aware of its contents, since it was forwarded from the main house, but could you tell her verbally that I intend to accept the meeting with Juumonji?" Tatsuya asked. "I'll forward a copy of my written response later."

"All right," Fumiya replied. "I'll see you later, Tatsuya."

"Sure. Thanks for stopping by."

Fumiya responded with a small smile, rather than a hug or a kiss on the cheek. Their farewell was not nearly that dramatic.

Around the time Tatsuya was speaking with Fumiya, Miyuki was hosting Ayako in her new Chofu flat.

"I heard you just moved on Monday, but everything seems so neat," Ayako noted politely as she sat on the reception room sofa across from Miyuki.

This apartment was much more spacious than the previous house, so there were rooms other than the living room specifically made for receiving guests.

"I didn't have much luggage, and Minami helped a lot," Miyuki explained. She looked up at Minami, who had just come in with a tray of tea and sweets.

"She seems quite capable for someone my age," Ayako complimented.

"Thank you," Minami said quietly with a humble bow.

Both she and Miyuki recognized Ayako's words as nothing more than a social nicety. After Minami finished serving, she disappeared behind a closed door. Miyuki and Ayako simultaneously turned to each other with tense smiles.

"Don't worry, Miyuki," Ayako began. "I'm simply a messenger today."

With neither Tatsuya nor Fumiya present to calm things down, the tension between the two girls was dangerously on the verge of escalating at any moment. Suddenly, Miyuki averted her gaze. Looking down at the table, she lifted her teacup in an admirably graceful way and took a sip of perfectly tempered tea. A few seconds later, Ayako delicately cut a piece of sweet bean jelly and brought it to her mouth. Miyuki waited until Ayako had swallowed to speak.

"Is the message you have from my aunt?" she asked.

"Yes, that's right," Ayako replied, setting down her fork without a sound.

"Let's hear it, then," Miyuki said.

"Recently, the National Defense Force has been attempting to abduct Tatsuya," Ayako said with a note of gravity.

"I see," Miyuki responded softly.

Despite Ayako's dramatic choice of words, Miyuki appeared remarkably calm.

"You don't seem surprised," Ayako noted in a tone that made it seem as if she had anticipated this reaction.

"That is because I'm not," Miyuki responded. "Unlike Tatsuya, I have never trusted the National Defense Force."

"I doubt Tatsuya's affiliation with the Independent Magic Battalion is solely based on trust," Ayako suggested.

"As true as that might be, feelings naturally develop from close relationships," Miyuki countered. "And Tatsuya has not been completely devoid of any emotions at all."

Ayako had not expected Miyuki to bring up Tatsuya's deficiency in emotions. She fell silent for a moment but quickly regained her composure and shifted back to the topic at hand.

"We will tell you the specifics regarding the date and time of the attack as soon as we find out, but that is all we can do," she stated.

"I'm not sure what you mean," Miyuki pressed.

"In other words, neither the main family nor the branch families can provide you or Tatsuya any support beyond information," Ayako explained.

"Is that my aunt's decision?"

"Yes."

"I see," Miyuki sighed.

Suddenly, the temperature of the entire room dropped several degrees. The tea on the table turned to ice and a frost developed on the surface of the sweet bean jelly. But the freeze didn't stop there. Tiny ice crystals even began to form on Ayako's clothes and hair.

"Ayako," Miyuki gently warned, her voice like softly falling snow. "You will freeze if you don't resist."

"I don't mind," Ayako responded with a resolute tone, though her lips trembled as their color drained. "Please continue until you're satisfied."

"All right," Miyuki whispered again, and the room's temperature immediately returned to normal.

A few seconds later, Minami came banging at the room's door.

"Miyuki, is everything okay?" she yelled on the other side.

"Come on in, Minami," Miyuki said.

"Thank you!"

As soon as Minami entered the room, she fell speechless. Condensation covered the entire area, though Miyuki's surroundings remained unaffected. Ayako sat across from Miyuki with her hair and clothes soaked through and her face noticeably pale.

"Minami," Miyuki said calmly, "could you guide Ayako to the bath? I will dry off this room."

"O-of course," Minami stammered. "This way, Miss Ayako."

Ayako obediently stood up and followed Minami before stopping at the door.

"Miyuki?" she ventured.

"Yes?" Miyuki replied coldly, without the slightest trace of guilt.

"You were exactly like Maya just now," Ayako said.

"I'm honored you think so," Miyuki replied.

"As I said, the Yotsuba clan will not be sending Tatsuya any aid. You're the only one who can help him."

With that, Ayako turned her back on Miyuki and walked out of the room.

"I'm aware of that," Miyuki replied. But by that time, Ayako was long gone.

"Are you sure you don't need any help, Miss Ayako?" Minami asked as they entered the bathroom. Ayako's footing was so precarious that she could barely stand, much less undress herself. Seeing this, anyone would have offered a helping hand.

"I appreciate your concern, but I'm fine," Ayako replied stubbornly.

"All right," Minami said uncertainly. "I will be here drying your clothes, so please feel free to call me if you need me."

Finally completely undressed, Ayako entered the bathroom and closed the door, which was not made of the typical frosted glass, but was a solid partition separating the bath and the changing room. Once in the bathing area, she could no longer be seen or heard. Ayako slipped to the floor of the tub, letting the shower run freely.

So that's Miyuki's power, she thought. *And that wasn't even her full strength.*

She had maintained her composure earlier out of pride, but now tears welled up in her eyes. The chilled air that had filled the reception room had not been an intentional spell; it had been a manifestation of uncontrolled magic power. Yet the low temperatures hadn't directly harmed Ayako's body. Naturally, Ayako's enhanced information capabilities had helped her protect herself to an extent. But Miyuki's magic, which should have been running wild, had just barely surrounded Ayako. The ice crystals that had formed in her hair hadn't been moisture that came from Ayako's body, but instead had come from the frozen moisture in the air that stuck to Ayako's form. The same was true about her clothes. Broadly speaking, her magic defenses were powerless against Miyuki's power.

Manipulation of reality is no simple feat, Ayako mused. *It was as if the world was bending to Miyuki's will. Her magic was like a supernatural charm that enslaved the natural order, placing it directly under her control.*

The thought made her shiver under the hot shower.

It was a Thursday afternoon in late May when Lieutenant Colonel Kazama of the Independent Magic Battalion received a call from Tatsuya while working at his desk.

"I'm sorry to bother you at such a busy time, Lieutenant Colonel. It's Tatsuya Shiba."

"Tatsuya," Kazama said, nodding. "Thank you for your help in Okinawa."

He recognized the significance of Tatsuya identifying himself by his real name over the phone. Though he served in the Independent

Magic Battalion as Specialist Ooguro, Tatsuya hinted he was making this call not as a member of the battalion but as a Yotsuba family magician.

"So what did you want to speak to me about today?" Kazama prompted.

"I heard the National Defense Force is planning an assault against me. Is this true?" Tatsuya asked in a tone as mechanical and cold as a robot's.

"It's not completely true," Kazama answered.

He didn't feel obligated to be completely honest, but for some reason, he couldn't bring himself to deny Tatsuya's question outright.

"Then how much is true?" Tatsuya pressed.

"It's the National Defense Force's Intelligence Department that has tabs on you," Kazama explained. "The potential assault you mentioned is an escalation of their intelligence operations, not a decision made by the military itself."

As he spoke, he briefly suspected an intervention of mental interference magic, but he quickly dismissed the possibility. It wasn't because Tatsuya could not use mental interference magic, but because Kazama felt somewhat guilty about Tatsuya's predicament. Besides, he felt speaking honestly to an extent would keep Tatsuya on the line.

"In other words, Intelligence is rebelling," Tatsuya said, his harsh words causing Kazama to pause before he spoke.

"...You could call it that," he replied after a while.

Ultimately, he had to admit Tatsuya wasn't wrong. Tatsuya's attack on a secret military facility had made him a criminal and, considering his status as a special officer, a rebel. However, the unauthorized use of state-entrusted military force was a grave offense. If they were to pass judgment on Tatsuya, the charges needed to first pass through a military court. As Tatsuya said, acting unilaterally without due process was undeniably an act of rebellion on the part of the Intelligence Department.

"In that case, as far as the battalion is concerned, there won't be an issue if I defend myself, right?" Tatsuya asked.

This time, Kazama found himself at a loss. The Intelligence Department's plan certainly went against both legal and military regulations. If this were to leak to the media, the military would face severe backlash, and the Cabinet would surely be forced to resign. It would be extremely beneficial if Tatsuya were to handle the matter discreetly. At the same time, it would be problematic for the 101st Battalion to appear to give approval for the annihilation of the Intelligence Department's execution squad.

In any organization with three or more members, there were inevitably going to be internal power struggles. The National Defense Force was no exception.

Under Major General Saeki's highly skilled leadership and impeccable career, the 101st Battalion fended off interference from bureaucrats and politicians. But in terms of factions, the battalion's foundation was weak. Despite her competence, Saeki faced resistance in the male-dominated organization, and she had very few pillars of support she could count on. Considering her position within the National Defense Force's power structure, it was crucial to minimize any potential vulnerabilities that could be exploited.

"Yes," Kazama finally answered, limiting the scope to an area where he could take responsibility if necessary, "there will be no problems as far as the Independent Magic Battalion is concerned."

He paused before continuing: "However, I hope you can understand we cannot offer you any support. You will need to overcome this with your own abilities."

"Of course," Tatsuya responded. *"I understand."*

For a moment, Kazama thought he saw an exceptionally cynical smile flash across Tatsuya's face.

"I'm glad we're on the same page," Tatsuya continued. *"Thank you for your time, Lieutenant Colonel."*

"Of course," Kazama replied. "Best of luck in battle. Or better yet, in general."

Tatsuya didn't need luck in battle. He would undoubtedly emerge victorious. Preventing the situation from worsening as a result of that victory, however, would take a stroke of general luck.

Kazama hung up the videophone before Tatsuya could respond. He dismissed the cynical smile he had seen as a figment of his imagination. His desk's videophone automatically recorded conversations. If he played back the call, he would quickly find out whether the derisive smile had been real or not. However, Kazama chose against this, immediately deleting the recorded data.

At lunchtime that Thursday, Mayumi approached Katsuto, who was sitting alone with a coffee at the Magic University's terrace coffee shop.

"Mind if I join you?" she asked.

"Of course not. Take a seat," Katsuto replied.

As she sat down, Katsuto realized she only had a single teacup on her tray.

"Did you eat lunch already?" he asked.

He had already finished his own lunch, but he had a tendency to eat quickly. Whenever sharing a meal, he adjusted his pace to the conversation. On his own, however, he finished his food swiftly. Today was no exception. He had moved from the cafeteria to the coffee shop right after lunch. Though Mayumi tended to eat less than he did, he doubted she could have finished so quickly.

"My third period class was canceled, so I had lunch in the cafeteria before it got crowded," Mayumi explained.

"Oh."

Magic University students were studious, and their schedules were always packed. Since Katsuto was no exception, he rarely had free time in the mornings. Afternoons tended to be more flexible, as a consideration for those who had household duties.

"Anyway, I came to ask you about what we talked about the other day," Mayumi said, jumping straight to the point. Anyone might think she was being hasty, but Katsuto knew she didn't like lingering in public spaces and drawing attention to herself.

Although she didn't specify exactly what she meant, she was clearly talking about the visit to Tatsuya's villa.

"I got a reply yesterday," Katsuto replied. "Everything will go as planned. I actually wanted to ask you if you were okay with leaving around 9 AM."

"Sure," Mayumi nodded, although a little surprised. "I guess that means we'll be meeting for lunch."

"We're dealing with a high schooler here," Katsuto explained. "It's not like we can meet him for drinks. Visiting him at night would just be a nuisance."

Despite Katsuto's logical reasoning, this wasn't exactly what had thrown Mayumi off guard.

"I just thought it might be better if we wait until it gets dark, since there's a possibility we might need to use force," she explained.

Despite the unsettling nature of her comment, Katsuto didn't silence her. Everyone around them knew Katsuto was the head of one of the Ten Master Clans and Mayumi was an heiress. It wasn't uncommon for a member of the Ten Master Clans to resort to force. Besides, the soundproof field around them minimized the worry that anyone was listening.

"Darkness raises the risk of unexpected mistakes," Katsuto replied, filling Mayumi with a mix of understanding and horror. It sounded like he was genuinely intent on crushing Tatsuya if he didn't comply.

"Juumonji," she said hesitantly, "it sounds like you're taking this more seriously than I thought."

"Of course I am," Katsuto responded firmly. "With someone like Tatsuya, I can't be anything but serious."

Wow... Mayumi thought, breaking into a cold sweat. *At this rate, not even my presence will stop them.*

During class on Friday, Miyuki couldn't stop thinking about the e-mail she had received from Ayako the night before. It contained information about the date and time the National Defense Force would be attacking Tatsuya. But this wasn't all. Ayako's e-mail also mentioned the military would be attacking in conjunction with Katsuto's visit.

That's two days from now, Miyuki thought. *If it were only the National Defense Force, Tatsuya could surely handle the situation. But if Juumonji gets involved...*

She shook her head.

In a one-on-one battle, I'm sure Tatsuya would win. The problem is, that's not what will be happening.

Miyuki clearly had a different perspective on Tatsuya and Katsuto's power dynamic than Mayumi. She never doubted her Tatsuya's strength and believed he was always the strongest. At the same time, she knew he was in no way invincible. If Katsuto teamed up with the National Defense Force, there was a real possibility of Tatsuya collapsing due to an overload in his magic-calculation region. Even if the two enemies did not form an alliance, Tatsuya might find himself considerably weakened if he fought Katsuto first and then had to weather an attack by the military.

I should go help him, Miyuki firmly decided while cleaning up after her student council duties.

Maya had never explicitly ordered Miyuki not to visit Tatsuya, but she had separated the two's living quarters. Going to help Tatsuya would undoubtedly be an act of defiance against their aunt.

Ayako had told Miyuki she was the only one who could help her fiancé, but this had just been a personal remark. Maya's actions overall implied she didn't want anyone to help Tatsuya. But for Miyuki, there was no other choice.

Of course, she thought. *There was never a need for hesitation from the very beginning.*

What Maya, the Yotsuba family, the National Defense Force, the nation, or even the world wanted didn't matter. Miyuki existed solely for Tatsuya. She knew what she had to do.

Miyuki, accompanied by the disciplinary committee duo Shizuku and Kasumi and freshmen Shiina and Saburou, was walking toward the station when she heard someone calling her from behind.

"Oh, hello, Erika," Miyuki greeted. "Are you all heading home, too? I thought everyone had already left, considering how late it is."

She and the other student council members had been working until just before the school gates closed. Though the days had become longer, it was already evening. Most students—including those involved in club activities—would have left the school by now.

"A patrol kicked us out," Erika replied nonchalantly.

"What Erika means to say," Mizuki corrected uncomfortably, "is that we were so engrossed in studying at the coffee shop terrace, we didn't realize how late it was."

Miyuki understood Mizuki's excuse completely. Regular exams at First High covered magic-related subjects and practical magic. General subjects were assessed through students' daily performance, rather than written exams. This was true from their freshman to senior years. While Mizuki was in the magic engineering course, which made her exam slightly different, Course 1 and 2 students took the same exams. So it wasn't surprising that Mikihiko, Erika, and Leo were studying together.

"You've never had study sessions before," Shizuku commented.

This wasn't entirely accurate. To be precise, the group had never had after-school study sessions before. But Leo ignored this minor detail.

"My grades have been improving lately, so I thought I'd take a shot at applying for the Magic University," he said a bit bashfully.

"I never really planned to go to university at all, but I thought it would be embarrassing if this idiot tried to get into the Magic University and I didn't," Erika added in her usual teasing way.

"Who are you calling an idiot?!" Leo yelled.

"Do you really think you're smart? That's presumptuous," Erika scoffed.

"All right, you two," Mizuki intervened. "That's enough of your lovers' quarrel for today."

Mikihiko, meanwhile, decided against jumping into dangerous territory.

"This isn't a lovers' quarrel!" Erika snapped back.

Mizuki ignored this and said, "You're so smart, Erika. I don't know why you didn't start studying sooner."

"Nice one, Shibata," Kasumi said with a nod of approval from her twin.

Realizing arguing with Mizuki's earlier comment would make her seem pathetic, Erika simply replied, "As I said before, I wasn't planning on going to college. I came to high school because my parents forced me to, but it ended up being the best decision in the end. So I guess I'm a little grateful for their nagging."

Mizuki giggled internally at Erika's shyness, which Erika of course intentionally ignored.

Mizuki giggled and said "You don't have to be embarrassed," which Erika of course pretended to not hear.

"What?" Mizuki said, surprised.

"A warrior-training trip?" Honoka asked hysterically.

"Yeah," Erika replied with a somewhat shy smile. "I want to focus on traditional martial arts rather than magic. I would take on a bunch of part-time jobs to earn money to support my trip. Then I'd start with visiting swordsmen across Japan and eventually travel the world. Or something like that."

Other than her, no one else was smiling.

"Can't you do that after graduating from college?" Miyuki asked.

"No way," Erika said, shaking her head. "I'll be too old by then."

"It doesn't matter how old you are," Miyuki insisted. "That is a wonderful goal. I could even help you, so that you wouldn't have to work, if Tatsuya agrees to it."

"I couldn't ask you to do that," Erika said, shaking her head even more fervently.

"I think it's a wonderful goal, too," Honoka chimed in.

"Same here," Shizuku added. "I'm more than happy to be another one of your sponsors."

"C-cut it out you guys," Erika insisted. Unable to handle all the attention any longer, she forcibly changed the subject. "Anyway, Miyuki, I was thinking of visiting Tatsuya this Sunday. Not alone, of course, but with everyone here. What do you think?"

"Oh, that's right!" Mizuki chimed in, suddenly remembering this was what they'd wanted to ask Miyuki from the very beginning. "We were talking about it during our study session."

"It's not that there's any particular reason we want to see him," Mikihiko said.

"We'd just like to see his face once in a while," Leo explained.

Miyuki felt her face turn crimson. Over the years, the Yotsuba family had used Tatsuya extensively—both for illegal activities and publicly as Taurus Silver. Tatsuya had even contributed significantly to the National Defense Force's efforts. It was thanks to him that they had been able to repel the Great Asian Alliance's army in October of the year before last.

Tatsuya had also done a lot to bolster First High's reputation. His victory in the previous Nine School Competition was undisputed. A considerable portion of the credit went to his efforts during the Nine School Competition in his freshman year as well. While he may not have won the Thesis Competition, the previous year's experiment he had produced was more than enough to compensate.

There may have been disagreements about the levels of Tatsuya's contributions, but his achievements were incontestable facts. Nevertheless, the Yotsuba family, the National Defense Force, and the school made no effort to protect him. In fact, the school seemed to even be taking the lead in attacking him.

Tatsuya's friends, on the other hand, were a different story. This was exactly why Miyuki couldn't allow them to get involved.

"I'm sorry, everyone," she politely declined, "Tatsuya has another guest visiting this Sunday."

She held back both her tears and any sign she wanted to cry, maintaining a solemn expression. Erika narrowed her eyes.

"Is this 'guest' someone who isn't welcome?" she asked.

Miyuki forced a smile and shook her head.

"No," she said. "I shouldn't be telling you this, but the guest is Juumonji."

Erika's slightly guilty expression seemed to stem from the remorse of forcing Miyuki into saying something she wasn't allowed to say.

"Huh," she huffed.

"So please don't do anything rash," Miyuki pleaded.

The look in her eyes gave Erika no choice but to obediently nod.

Raymond S. Clark, a boy who comically called himself one of the "Seven Sages," was in a bad mood these days. The cause was his inability to play his favorite game with the Hlidskjalf.

It wasn't that the Hlidskjalf was broken. His terminal, at least, was functioning as usual. It was the terminals of the other six users that had stopped working. More precisely, the system administrator had shut them down. As a result, Raymond had lost the thrill of peeking at the information the other users collected.

But this wasn't the only issue at hand. Now that he was the only one who could use a system akin to clairvoyance, the excitement of the game was spoiled. No matter what he did, there were no penalties for his actions. Peeping and eavesdropping at will were entirely within his power. It was as if he were playing alone in a child's fantasy. And that wasn't fun at all.

Raymond had pleaded with his father, Edward Clark—Hlidskjalf's developer and administrator—to restore the rights to the other users. But Edward had shook his head. "Wait awhile" was all his father had said.

But Raymond didn't protest. He was obedient enough to give up after one try. In the meantime, he searched for a new way to play—a method that produced more thrills and excitement.

Among all the games Raymond had played with the Hlidskjalf, taking the role of adviser during the Vampire Incident had excited him the most. He had played the roles of accuser and escapee before, but he had never felt the sense of being a direct participant so keenly as he had during that incident. He yearned to experience that exhilaration again. Or something even greater.

Now that the thrill of using Hlidskjalf had diminished due to the reduction of risks, Raymond decided he would take risks voluntarily. To this day, he had never revealed his true identity in any situation except one.

With the exception of that one time, he had completely avoided the risk of having his identity discovered. But Raymond decided it was time to break this streak. Of course, this didn't mean he planned to go out into the world with his real face carelessly exposed. He wanted to experiment with the limits of how much he could disguise his appearance, mechanically change his voice, and deceive others.

Angie Sirius, one of the USNA's Thirteen Apostles, used magic to change her appearance. Raymond wondered how much he could transform himself with the power of the Hlidskjalf's system. His childish curiosity could no longer be suppressed.

[8]

A group of unexpected guests arrived at Tatsuya's villa on Saturday night. Knowing the notification couldn't be mistaken, Tatsuya stood up from his workstation and went to the front entrance to welcome them.

A large sedan with tinted glass concealing its passengers came to a smooth stop in the driveway. As a young man stepped out from the driver's seat, a girl emerged almost simultaneously from the left rear seat.

The young man was Hyougo Hanabishi, and the girl was Minami Sakurai. Minami maintained a graceful pose as she held open the back door. Hyougo greeted Tatsuya with a somewhat reserved smile. Then it happened.

A mystically beautiful girl stepped out of the car, assisted by Minami's hand. Her elegant black hair blew in the wind as she lifted her face, and her eyes met Tatsuya's.

"Tatsuya!" Miyuki cried, jumping into her brother's arms.

"I wasn't expecting you," Tatsuya whispered into Miyuki's ear while gently embracing her fragile frame.

"I missed you so much," she said.

"As did I. But you're treating me like your brother again."

Miyuki hesitated before reluctantly pulling away from Tatsuya's arms. She had completely forgotten Hyougo was present. Even if he weren't around, one never knew who was watching or listening.

"...It has been too long, Tatsuya," she corrected herself, bowing respectfully.

"I know," Tatsuya agreed. "Even though only a week has passed, it feels like it's been an eternity."

Tatsuya arranged for Hyougo to pick up Miyuki and Minami the next evening before guiding the two girls to the villa. Each of them had no more than a small bag. In addition to Tatsuya's personal items, the villa had also been prepared with clothes for both girls.

When Miyuki had told Minami about this as they'd been preparing for their visit, Minami had made a face. She didn't like the thought of her clothes being in a place out of her reach, and it didn't help that a member of the opposite sex was near them. While she didn't actually think Tatsuya would rummage through her underwear, she still felt uneasy about it. Miyuki, on the other hand, didn't seem to mind at all.

As soon as they entered the villa, Pixie promptly took their two small bags. More precisely, a nonhumanoid porter robot controlled by Pixie carried the bags away. Now that they no longer needed to stop by their bedrooms, Miyuki and Minami sat down on the living room sofa with Tatsuya.

"I'm sure you haven't had dinner yet," he said. "I'll have it prepared right away."

Just as he spoke, Minami jumped out of her seat.

"I can cook," she volunteered. Though her voice was calm, there was a fiery passion in her eyes that was raring to get started.

"Okay," Tatsuya relented. "Pixie, switch kitchen system to manual mode."

"Request. Declined," Pixie replied abruptly.

It would have made sense if she had said she couldn't fulfill the task, although this would be a blatant lie. Tatsuya knew Pixie was capable of switching to manual mode. But to be fair, she could be experiencing a malfunction.

Disobeying her owner's orders, on the other hand, was against machine protocol. Though impressed by Pixie's intelligence, Tatsuya gave the command again.

"You can't decline my request, Pixie. Switch kitchen system to manual mode. That's an order."

"Master," she replied. "Do you prefer. That human's cooking. To mine?"

Tatsuya felt a migraine coming on. There was no doubt about it. Pixie's self-awareness had been growing since he had arrived at the Izu villa. While she had taken initiative to take care of things before Tatsuya gave her instructions, this was the first time she had actively defied his orders. It was much too dangerous to let her get away with it.

"This doesn't have anything to do with my preferences," Tatsuya said firmly. "Now do as you're told."

"Yes, Master," Pixie seemed to grumble. Tatsuya thought this must be his imagination, since she wasn't programmed to even have discontent. After a brief pause, she obediently switched the kitchen system to manual mode.

"Thank you," Tatsuya said. "Now go into standby."

"Yes, Master," she replied.

Again, the objection in her voice was almost certainly Tatsuya's imagination. Pixie settled into a chair in the corner of the room and became motionless like a doll. Meanwhile, Minami cheerfully scurried into the kitchen.

"I won!" she whispered on her way, but both Tatsuya and Miyuki chose to ignore this.

Minami prepared dinner, served both Tatsuya and Miyuki, and cleaned up the dishes. Once she had prepared a bath and made the beds, she was finally satisfied. So Tatsuya released Pixie from her standby mode with some hesitation to deal with the remaining tasks. There wasn't much left to do other than some security protocol, but Pixie didn't complain.

Of course not, Tatsuya thought, scolding himself for even thinking she would.

He turned his gaze to Miyuki, who was relaxing on the other side of the table. The two were on the balcony, where a table had been set up for them to sit facing each other. A nonhumanoid robot had set it up. While the villa was home to many robots, Pixie was the only humanoid type.

It was already past 9 PM by the time they finished their meal. Despite their light clothing, it wasn't too cold outside. The villa may be in the mountains, but it was also on the Izu Peninsula, and it was late May. The temperature was just right, and the occasional breeze was more refreshing than anything they could experience in the city.

Miyuki smiled as a gentle wind blew through her hair. She had been bothered by the tension between Minami and Pixie until a moment ago. Luckily, sitting on the balcony helped to lighten her mood.

"This is such a nice place," she said.

"Isn't it?" Tatsuya replied. "It's the perfect place for a temporary getaway."

In the darkness of the night, the light seeping from indoors highlighted Miyuki's fair skin. Her silky black hair scattered like stars with every gust of wind, and her black, pearl-like eyes shimmered with a light from within. As Tatsuya stared at her intently, his sense of reality began to fade. It was almost as if Miyuki was not of this world. Her ethereal beauty made her seem something other than human; a celestial—even magical—being.

"You know…it's a little embarrassing when you stare at me like that," she said.

Tatsuya suddenly snapped back to reality. Miyuki lowered her gaze and blushed, her fingers fiddling restlessly on her lap. Tatsuya suddenly grasped that he had been staring.

"Sorry," he replied. "You're just so mesmerizing."

"Wh-what is that supposed to mean?" Miyuki said, turning more crimson by the second.

Tatsuya realized he couldn't control his impulses. Maybe he had missed Miyuki more than she had missed him. In a rare moment, he struggled to keep his emotions in check. At the same time, he envied those who did not have to put limits on such intense feelings of joy.

"I'm really sorry," he repeated. "I'll do anything to make it up to you. Please just let me see your face."

"All right," Miyuki said shyly.

Something must have revealed itself in her tone of voice. As Tatsuya stared deep into her eyes, he realized something.

"Did you come here because you know what's going to happen tomorrow?" he asked.

"Yes," she replied. She took a breath and then asked him back, "Are you aware Juumonji will not be alone tomorrow?"

"Yes," he said. "Fumiya told me."

"I see," she said, followed by a brief silence.

"Miyuki," Tatsuya began. "I don't want to put you in danger."

"I know," she said. There was another brief silence before she continued, "I do not plan to get in the way of your fight with Juumonji."

"Juumonji and I are only going to talk," Tatsuya insisted.

"We both know it will not stop there," Miyuki said.

"Yeah..." Tatsuya sighed. "You're probably right."

He was more woeful than annoyed at this inevitable conclusion. Tatsuya recognized Katsuto as a formidable opponent and preferred not to fight him if possible.

"Tatsuya?" Miyuki ventured.

"Yeah?"

"Juumonji will probably use his secret weapon."

"That would only risk shortening his life," Tatsuya countered.

The two had only recently learned about the Juumonji family trump card. When Katsuto had blocked Tatsuya from attacking

Tsukasa Tooyama, they had realized a clash with him was unavoidable. So they had dug into the Juumonji family's secrets with Maya's help.

"It would also result in a difficult battle in your current state," Miyuki insisted.

"Miyuki," Tatsuya warned, "have you received Aunt Maya's permission?"

He sensed she was planning something that went beyond her words.

"No," she said. "It's my own decision."

"Cut it out," he pressed. "My battle with Juumonji is personal. Convincing Maya to allow you to intervene won't be easy."

"We don't need her approval," Miyuki contended. "I want to do it, so I will take full responsibility."

"Calm down," Tatsuya said.

"I am perfectly calm, Tatsuya," Miyuki replied with a sadness in her eyes powerful enough to silence her fiancé—and her brother.

"In the end," she continued, "I am no more than your little sister. It was not until I became the Yotsuba family heiress and you became Aunt Maya's son that we were able to get engaged. In fact, it was the only way…"

Miyuki trailed off for only a moment to suppress a rising sob.

"I hate to make Aunt Maya angry, but I also can't stand to see you get hurt," she continued calmly. "I want to completely and utterly remove your seal."

"What do you mean?" Tatsuya asked, recognizing Miyuki's careful choice of words.

"Exactly what it sounds like," she said firmly. "I no longer want you to be bound by the shackles others have imposed on you."

"Hold on." Tatsuya panicked, rising from his seat. "I know it's not impossible, but—"

"The caster bears a significant burden in the process," Miyuki said, finishing his sentence. "In other words, it's the one who placed the seal rather than the one who has been sealed who suffers, correct?"

The determination in her voice made Tatsuya return to his seat. Tatsuya's Material Burst was sealed by the mental interference spell called Oath, which had been cast by the Tsukuba family, a Yotsuba family branch. The caster herself was Touka Tsukuba, the head of the Tsukuba family. Oath not only sealed Tatsuya's most powerful weapon, but it also restricted his magic power to about half of its full potential. In other words, it was a spell that prohibited specific active decisions and limited magic as a side effect.

The most unique aspect of the spell was that it could use magic power other than the caster's to sustain the effects of mental interference. It was meaningless to try to prohibit something if that restriction was only effective in front of the caster. A prison guard couldn't watch over a single prisoner all hours of the day. Moreover, having a single magician control one person would be incredibly inefficient.

This was why Oath was typically maintained by enchanting either the target or a third party connected to the target. If the restrictions on the target's decision-making were semipermanent, the target was usually the one who was enchanted. In cases that required a temporary lifting of restrictions, a third party connected to the target could contribute their magic power.

In the latter case, the third party received a key of sorts to temporarily lift the seal. With that key, the original caster's prohibitions would temporarily disappear. To return those prohibitions to their original state, either the original caster or the holder of the key had to perform a ritual to trigger the reactivation.

Miyuki was the one who held the key to Tatsuya's seal. As long as she did not perform the reactivation ritual, Tatsuya's seal would remain lifted. But it would still be considered temporary. Miyuki would need to continue to supply magic power to Oath, gradually making the seal more powerful, which would put Tatsuya in a dangerous situation if left unattended.

It was impossible for Touka Tsukuba to control Tatsuya's Material Burst with her magic alone. Therefore, a supplementary arrangement had been added to Oath when it was cast on Tatsuya. Miyuki's magic control was used to bind Tatsuya's magic-calculation region. In other words, it was as if Tatsuya and Miyuki shared the Oath seal. Miyuki's own Oath, which she had cast on herself, was maintained by her own magic and could be temporarily lifted with the key she possessed.

Under this system, if the magic supply connecting Miyuki to the seal was interrupted, the magical effects would naturally disappear in a matter of seconds. However, this also meant the Oath written in her consciousness would cause her distress.

Miyuki's claim that the caster bore a significant burden in this case wasn't completely accurate. Although Touka was the one who had cast Oath in the first place, Miyuki would be the one who suffered, since she had been forced to supply magic to the spell and maintain the seal.

"I appreciate you wanting to make sure I'm in perfect condition for this battle," Tatsuya said. "But a temporary release of the seal is enough. There's no need to suffer the risks that come with lifting Oath completely."

"You don't understand," Miyuki responded. "I can't bear it anymore that I'm part of the shackles that bind you. I hate that you have to endure so much pain because of me."

The way she spoke had reverted to how she had prior to New Year's Eve. She clearly couldn't stand the situation any longer.

Although the Yotsuba family claimed to genuinely welcome him into the family, they were quick to abandon him when push came to shove. They did provide him with information, but this only meant so much. The information only proved useful when Tatsuya was forced to respond to impending disaster. It was no different than notifying someone that their city was under a missile attack but refusing to provide any protection or aid.

Tatsuya wasn't your average powerless citizen, of course. He was strong and had ways to fight back. However, there were still limits to what a single person could do.

The Yotsuba family also had the power to support him. There was a reason outsiders considered them untouchable. They should be strong enough to resist the nation. Yet they kept Tatsuya in chains, expecting him to fight alone. This harsh treatment angered Miyuki from the bottom of her heart. Enough was enough.

"If Aunt Maya wants you to fend for yourself," Miyuki began, flames of colorless intensity burning in her jet-black eyes deeper than the clear night sky, "I will make sure you can wield your true power."

Miyuki stood from her chair and walked over to Tatsuya.

"All right," he relented, standing too.

But he didn't get down on his knees for her to perform the ritual. Instead, he said, "But I want to prepare first. Follow me."

He turned his back on Miyuki and led the way inside the villa.

"O-okay," she stammered.

Miyuki felt as if her enthusiasm had been completely ignored, but she obediently followed. The two walked into the living room, where Minami and Pixie were waiting.

"Minami," Tatsuya said to get her attention and request "I'd like you to take a bath with Miyuki."

The unexpected instruction made Miyuki's eyes widen.

What does bathing have to do with what we just discussed? she wondered.

"You mean...you want us to bathe together?" Minami clarified with a bewildered look, echoing Miyuki's feelings exactly.

"Yes," Tatsuya affirmed. "The bath here is spacious enough for the two of you. Wash Miyuki well, but avoid using any products with a strong fragrance."

"All...right," Minami replied, confused.

"Pixie will prepare a change of clothes when you're done," he added.

"And you would like Miyuki to wear that?" Minami asked.

"Yes."

"Understood. Come with me, Miyuki."

Minami didn't understand why Tatsuya was telling her to do this, but an order was an order. Besides, she enjoyed taking care of Miyuki whenever the opportunity arose. Miyuki usually rejected any offers of help in the bath and bedroom, so she used Tatsuya's instructions as an excuse to serve. Miyuki was lost in a fog of confusion as she was led to the bathroom.

After scrubbing Miyuki up and down, Minami placed her into the bathtub and quickly finished her own bath. Miyuki seemed somewhat exhausted, but Minami savored the fulfilling moment.

When they exited the bathroom, they found a surprising outfit neatly laid out for Miyuki to wear. Miyuki reached out to touch what was usually the uniform for a shrine maiden.

"Minami," she said hesitantly, "is this a white kimono?"

"Yes, it is," Minami replied.

"And this looks like a scarlet *hakama*," Miyuki said with just as much perplexity.

"It does," Minami agreed.

"There doesn't seem to be a singlet or underskirt," Miyuki noticed. "Does that mean I should wear the clothes without anything underneath?"

"That seems to be what Tatsuya wants," Minami replied.

"Hmm," Miyuki murmured, but she resigned herself to her fate and donned the white kimono directly on her pale skin.

The fabric felt unexpectedly soft and comfortable. Next, she pulled the crimson *hakama* up over the robe. The long garment reached down to her ankles, and she felt a bit embarrassed to be wearing it without any underwear.

Once the two girls emerged from the changing room, Tatsuya entered the bath. While he was bathing, Miyuki and Minami took turns drying their hair. Miyuki's long hair required some time to dry properly, and she was careful not to use any products with fragrance.

By the time they were finished with their hair, Tatsuya had completed his bath.

"Miyuki, are you done?" he called out.

"Yes, you can come in," she replied, standing up from the seat in front of her mirror and turning toward the door.

Tatsuya stepped into the room dressed in a white kimono and matching *hakama*. The outfit didn't sport any crests or decorations; it was just a plain white.

"Follow me. Minami, you're free to take a break now."

Without another word of explanation, Tatsuya walked out of the room. Miyuki and Minami exchanged glances and did as they were told.

Tatsuya led Miyuki to a Japanese-style room. A square vermilion carpet had been laid out on the tatami mats, with piles of salt at each corner. In the center of the carpet was a white wooden altar with a white bottle and two porcelain cups on top. Tatsuya knelt in front of the small altar, folding both of his legs underneath him.

"Take a seat," he instructed.

Miyuki obediently did as she was told, sitting on the other side of the altar.

"Let me explain to you about Oath," he said suddenly.

Miyuki straightened her posture, preparing to listen intently.

"In a technical sense, the Tsukuba family's Oath is a ritual that compels its target to use magic of the caster's choice. In other words, it forces its target to employ magic that manipulates the mind. You could say it intervenes in the magic process itself. That's why its effectiveness is limited unless the target is a magician."

Miyuki nodded.

"Oath's ability to intervene in the magic process sets it deep within the target's consciousness, near a gate," Tatsuya continued. "Therefore, its system is similar to Gatekeeper."

"You mean the Gatekeeper you developed?" Miyuki asked.

"That's right," Tatsuya confirmed. "Oath is a ritual that forces the use of magic, while Gatekeeper is a ritual that prevents the use of magic. It's natural for the two systems to be similar."

Miyuki nodded again.

"This also means Gatekeeper should be able to erase Oath completely," Tatsuya said.

He took a cup from the wooden altar and offered it to Miyuki. She took it hesitantly. Tatsuya then lifted the lid from the white bottle with his free hand and faced its spout toward Miyuki.

"I don't understand," she said.

"Don't worry. It's not alcohol," Tatsuya reassured her.

But her confusion didn't come from a misunderstanding that Tatsuya was offering her alcohol. This felt like some kind of ritual. Like a traditional Japanese marriage ceremony. Although the latter involved three cups of different sizes, the ambience was eerily similar. Miyuki timidly held out her cup, and Tatsuya poured a clear liquid into it. As Miyuki brought the cup closer to her face, she noticed the liquid had no smell. With a determined breath, she drank the liquid in a single gulp. A confused look spread across her face. The liquid had no taste.

"What was that?" she asked.

"Highly purified water," Tatsuya explained. "I couldn't make it ultrapure because of the container and environmental factors, but the lack of impurities means it's close enough."

He handed the bottle to Miyuki. She took it and poured water into Tatsuya's cup.

"Is it supposed to symbolize parting?" she asked, her voice and hands trembling slightly.

"Of course not," Tatsuya replied as he emptied his cup as well. "If that were the case, I wouldn't have gone to the trouble of preparing such pure water."

"I guess not," Miyuki said, her trembling coming to a stop.

Tatsuya returned his cup to the wooden altar. Miyuki followed suit with both the bottle and porcelain cup.

"This was a ritual to purify ourselves," Tatsuya explained. "It's only symbolic, of course, but by imbibing pure substances, we elevate the purity of our bodies and minds. I wanted a pure consumable substance that wouldn't harm us, and water was the most accessible thing."

He moved the wooden altar aside, eliminating anything that stood between himself and Miyuki before continuing.

"If we want to come in contact with Oath in the deepest parts of our consciousness, we must also make a profound connection."

"What?" Miyuki said wide-eyed. Surely, he was joking.

"What's wrong?" Tatsuya asked.

"Oh!" Miyuki gasped as Tatsuya met her with a completely serious gaze. She felt her consciousness start to slip away and her cheeks turn bright red.

"I-I just thought..." she murmured softly, "our first time would be in a bed."

With her face in her hands and embarrassment painted on her entire form, Tatsuya could barely hear her. It took him a minute to understand what she meant, but when he did, his entire expression froze.

"I'm so sorry!" he said, pressing his forehead to the tatami mat with a loud thump.

"F-for what?" Miyuki asked, hesitantly lowering her hands from her face.

"That didn't come out right at all," Tatsuya said in a panic, raising his head from the floor. For what seemed like the first time, his eyes were brimming with embarrassment.

"I meant a profound connection in the psychological sense," he explained. "In this case, any physical intimacy would actually, um, interfere with the process, as that involves sharing a life force."

It took a second for Tatsuya's words to sink in. Realizing her mistake, Miyuki covered her face in embarrassment again and tried to flee from the room. Before she was successful, Tatsuya swiftly reached out and grabbed her upper arm.

"Let me go!" she squealed. "I beg of you!"

"Please calm down," he pleaded. "This was all my fault."

If he let go now, he knew the awkwardness between them would simply drag on. Driven by his intuition, he desperately tried to convince Miyuki to stay.

Ultimately, Tatsuya's persuasion worked, and Miyuki regained her composure in a matter of minutes.

"I apologize for behaving so poorly," she said.

"That's okay," Tatsuya replied, gazing into Miyuki's eyes. "I'm the one responsible for the mix-up."

The two blushed with embarrassment and gradually turned serious again.

"Well, then. Let's get started," Miyuki proposed, breaking the brief silence.

"Right," Tatsuya nodded, slowly moving closer to his fiancée.

Once their knees were touching, they met each other's gaze once more.

"I'll explain the plan," Tatsuya said.

"All right," Miyuki replied.

"Once the seal is lifted, I want you to stop supplying magic to Oath."

"Right."

"When that happens, Oath's program will become more active to try to fulfill its pledge, and the main spell hidden within the depths of our consciousness will reveal itself."

"Okay."

"At that moment, I'll shoot at it with Gatekeeper. I won't be able to touch it when it's mixed with our consciousness, since I can't perform mental interference magic. But I *can* disassemble it when its magic program has been exposed."

"All right. I'll do what I can."

Meeting Tatsuya's gaze, Miyuki rose to her knees. Placing her hands on Tatsuya's shoulders, she pressed her lips against his forehead. Psion light surged. Within a raging storm of psions, Miyuki's strength began to leave her hands. Tatsuya supported her by grabbing her waist. He could feel the softness and warmth of her body through the thin fabric of the white kimono, but he remained unfazed. He knew he had to concentrate on the task at hand. Holding Miyuki's trembling form in his arms, he directed his Elemental Sight into Miyuki's consciousness.

The psyche was not a realm Tatsuya's "eyes" could reach. He endured the pain of almost burning out from the excessive concentration and tried to see that which was not usually visible. He dived within Miyuki's consciousness in an effort to spot magic that was not hers.

After a few moments, he finally found it. He used his Elemental Sight to focus on Oath's exposed program and cast Gatekeeper. Tatsuya's ability to target the program's gate—the exit through which magic programs were ejected into the subconscious realm—came from Program Dispersion.

Program Dispersion was a spell that was anathema to other magic, as it was capable of breaking down the very information bodies they were made of. Even magic that influenced the mind was not composed of psions, but rather of psionic information bodies. This made it susceptible to Program Dispersion. Once Oath exposed itself by fulfilling its pledge and laid its essence bare, it was completely eradicated by Tatsuya's spell.

And with that, Tatsuya gained his freedom.

[9]

As promised, Katsuto pulled up to the Saegusa family driveway to pick up Mayumi on Sunday morning. In terms of size, power, and durability, Katsuto's car was impeccable. But to Mayumi, it looked like the kind of vehicle used to enter conflict zones in Central Asia.

"Did you get this from the National Defense Force or something?" she asked in disbelief.

"No," Katsuto replied, confused. "It's just a regular car."

His SUV was not a custom-made model or even a fully customized vehicle. It was what people called a special works car, which was a limited-production model fine-tuned from its original. Its original design was essentially that of a detuned military vehicle, but as Katsuto claimed, it was a regular car.

After being subjected to unjust suspicions, Katsuto had his own comment for Mayumi.

"On another note," he said, his eyes narrowing more than usual, "you never told me Watanabe was coming."

This felt like déjà vu from the café meeting they had had with Miyuki and Tatsuya in April.

You tell her, Juumonji, Mari seemed to say with her eyes as she stood next to Mayumi.

A perfect apologetic smile spread across Mayumi's lips.

"Never mind," Katsuto sighed. "I get it. You're worried about your poor underclassman."

"Hey!" Mari protested. "No one said I'm here by choice!"

But her wandering eyes told a different story.

"Silly Mari," Mayumi said coyly. "You don't have to be shy about it."

"For goodness' sake," she sighed, and she gave up saying more.

"Anyway, let's get a move on!" Mayumi urged. "We're on a schedule here."

"Right," Katsuto said.

Although they didn't have any other plans besides visiting Tatsuya, arguing like this was only a waste of time. With that thought in mind, Katsuto returned to the driver's seat. Mayumi slid cheerfully into the back seat, and Mari followed with a resigned look on her face.

Mayumi had begun the trip to Izu in high spirits, but her enthusiasm had taken a nosedive once they'd arrived at their destination.

"I can't agree to that," Tatsuya stated matter-of-factly to Katsuto.

The two young men were seated across from each other in the villa's reception room. Miyuki was next to Tatsuya with an inscrutable expression on her face, while Mayumi was next to Katsuto. Since the beginning of their meeting, Mayumi had felt the pressure of Miyuki's gaze, making it difficult to maintain a polite smile.

"Why not?" Katsuto asked solemnly back to Tatsuya.

Mayumi was almost jumping out of her seat with anxiety. But neither Tatsuya nor Miyuki showed any signs of being bothered.

"I could ask you the same thing," Tatsuya contended. "Why do you think I should join the Dione Project?"

"Shiba," Katsuto said patiently. "Two years ago, I said you should join the Ten Master Clans."

"Yes, I remember," Tatsuya replied.

"The Ten Master Clans are an element Sage Kudou created as part of a mutual aid system for the magicians of this country," Katsuto began.

"They're more like the managers of the mutual aid system in my opinion," Tatsuya corrected. "But go on."

"I believe those who possess great power or exceptional abilities also bear great responsibility," Katsuto said.

This time, Tatsuya remained silent, waiting for Katsuto's next words.

"The majority of magicians don't possess much power," Katsuto continued. "In fact, most of them can't even compete with ordinary, citizens who have martial arts and combat training but no magic."

"I believe that depends on the individual," Tatsuya argued. "Besides, unless magicians serve in the military or police force, they are no different than ordinary citizens."

"Way to be argumentative…" Mari murmured next to Mayumi in exasperation.

Both Tatsuya and Katsuto ignored her comment.

"However," Katsuto carried on, "it is still true non-magicians consider magicians a dangerous race, not only in this country but all over the world."

"Not everyone thinks that way, but we don't have to worry about that right now," Tatsuya said, and he gestured for Katsuto to continue.

"I don't disagree with the idea that magicians are fundamentally different from humans. However, we must not forget the fact that magicians are a minority within the human race," Katsuto stated. "This is why magicians need to help one another and why Sage Kudou rightly created the Ten Master Clans."

"I agree with that as long as magicians' mutual aid doesn't lead to disdain and exclusion toward non-magicians," Tatsuya expressed.

"Are you suggesting magicians consider themselves an elite class and look down on non-magicians?" Mari interjected, implying Tatsuya was overthinking.

"I'm just saying it's not an impossible future scenario," Tatsuya responded instead of ignoring her this time.

Katsuto, on the other hand, ignored both Mari's question and Tatsuya's response.

"Shiba," he said, "I'm asking you to become a member of the Ten Master Clans and extend a helping hand to your fellow magicians."

"Mr. Juumonji, I apologize for speaking out of turn, but Tatsuya is already related directly to the Yotsuba clan head," Miyuki said, speaking up for the first time.

The night before, she had discussed with Tatsuya in full about presenting themselves in this meeting as engaged and referring to Tatsuya in a polite manner.

"Yes, I'm aware he will be the next Yotsuba clan head," he said directly to Miyuki. Then turning to Tatsuya: "But I believe being a member of the Ten Master Clans is a job, not a birthright. Magicians with great power should assist those who are weaker. In the current public opinion, magicians are increasingly running out of breathing room. Baseless accusations that we are starting wars are openly being shared in the forum of public opinion."

Katsuto paused to see how Tatsuya would react. But noticing the younger boy maintain his poker face, he continued.

"But I don't blame you for the strategic magic incident, Shiba. If you ask me, you're completely blameless."

This *strategic magic incident* referred to Shiba's spell, Active Air Mine, being used by an armed guerrilla in Central Asia. The incident had caused significant ripples among Magic High School students and even led to the Nine School Competition's cancellation. But Tatsuya had never felt a shred of guilt for that incident, so he remained unfazed by Katsuto's comment. Katsuto realized his miscalculation and continued to speak.

"In any case," he began, "your participation in the Dione Project can help us convince people that magic is not only for war. Now that the New Soviet Union has announced their involvement in the project, Japan is falling behind in the movement toward the peaceful use of magic. Don't you understand? We can't overlook the defamation and slander against domestic magicians any longer. We need to do something."

"I hear your concerns, Mr. Juumonji," Miyuki interjected again. "But why Tatsuya? There are world-famous professors at the Magic University who can easily take his place."

Katsuto didn't have an immediate answer to Miyuki's question. He knew it was rational to argue national issues shouldn't be placed on the shoulders of a high school student. Nevertheless, driven by a sense of duty as the head of one of the Ten Master Clans, he wanted to respond.

Before he could say a word, Mayumi intervened. Feeling it was unfair to leave Katsuto speaking the entire time, she thought she would at least deal with Miyuki to lighten his load.

"Isn't it obvious, Miyuki?" she said. "It's because Tatsuya is Taurus Silver, who Edward Clark personally invited onto the project."

"What?!" Mari exclaimed, more surprised than anyone else present.

Miyuki simply frowned. Meanwhile, Tatsuya still maintained his usual poker face.

"Even if Tatsuya *were* Taurus Silver," Miyuki said quietly, "what difference would it make?"

"Wh-what do you mean?" Mayumi asked in surprise, clearly not having expected this answer.

"Even if Tatsuya were Taurus Silver," Miyuki repeated, "it doesn't change the fact that he is a high schooler and a minor."

Mayumi remained silent.

"Besides," Miyuki added, "the Yotsuba clan has already refused to acknowledge Tatsuya and Taurus Silver are one and the same."

Her statement implied if anyone insisted on claiming Tatsuya was Taurus Silver, it might lead to a full-scale confrontation with the Yotsuba clan. In other words, Miyuki was prepared to stand against both the Saegusa and Juumonji clans. Mayumi, on the other hand, did not feel comfortable with being the one to pull the trigger on any sort of conflict between her family and Miyuki's. This was the difference between the two young women.

"Shiba," Katsuto said, breaking the chilly silence. "Are you really saying you won't participate in the project no matter what?"

"That's right," Tatsuya nodded. "The Dione Project has an ulterior motive I can't agree with."

"Are you saying you believe it's trying to push magicians out of this country for malicious reasons?" Katsuto inquired.

"You can put it that way, yes," Tatsuya replied.

Imaginary sparks of tension flew between the two young men.

"Fine. I didn't want it to come to this, but you leave me no choice," Katsuto said, standing up from his seat. "Meet me outside, Shiba."

Tatsuya also stood up and met Katsuto's gaze.

"Are you sure about this?" he asked.

Either Mayumi or Mari swallowed a scream as a chill filled the air. But this time, Miyuki's magic wasn't the cause.

"These are desperate times," Katsuto said. "I can't allow you to back out now."

Either Miyuki or Minami let out a frustrated huff. A crushing force that felt as if the Earth's gravity had been multiplied several times over emanated from Katsuto's body.

"Fine by me," Tatsuya said, completely disposing of all formalities. "Pixie, bring me my CAD."

"Yes, Master," the robot said and obediently carried over the CAD in its case.

"I'll meet you out there," Katsuto said, turning his back on Tatsuya.

He had absolutely no fear of being attacked from behind.

"Saegusa, Watanabe," Tatsuya said somewhat gently now that the two girls had been released from pulling the trigger. "I'm sure you have better places to be. You are free to leave when you wish."

"Is it okay if we back up Juumonji?" Mayumi asked.

"Isn't that what you've been doing this whole time?" Tatsuya said coldly.

"You sound pretty confident," Mari scoffed. "I hope you don't regret this."

"I won't," Tatsuya responded with the same cold tone. "No matter how it ends."

"Let's go, Mari," Mayumi said. She stood up, urging her friend to do the same.

"Fine," Mari replied. "But Tatsuya, don't forget what you said."

With that, the two girls followed Katsuto out the villa's front door.

When Tatsuya walked outside with Miyuki and Minami, he found Katsuto, Mayumi, and Mari standing stiffly in front of the SUV. Tatsuya walked up to Katsuto before completely passing the older young man.

"Follow me," Tatsuya explained. "I don't want to damage the house."

After Miyuki and Minami passed by, Katsuto followed behind them. Mayumi and Mari, meanwhile, hurriedly followed Katsuto.

A pair of eyes observed Tatsuya and Katsuto from the shadows of the trees. Once they confirmed that Mari, who was at the group's rear, had moved far enough away, the watcher brought his wristwatch close to his lips.

"Mouse here. Tatsuya Shiba has left the villa. He seems to be headed toward the abandoned golf course, over."

A part of the wristwatch served as the microphone for a communication device.

"Boar here. Copy that. Cease surveillance and regroup with the main unit, over."

A built-in speaker in Mouse's glasses delivered the response from the other side.

"Don't you want me to confirm their destination? Over," Mouse asked.

"No need to take any unnecessary risks to tail them," Boar replied. *"Monkey is stationed at the abandoned golf course and Bird is in the other direction, over."*

"Copy that. Mouse out."

The man who went by the codename Mouse was a spy belonging to the National Defense Force's Special Affairs Section. The unit planning to attack Tatsuya mainly consisted of personnel from the Counterintelligence Unit, which included Tsukasa Tooyama. But to ensure Tatsuya remained in their sight, the Special Affairs Section had also been assigned surveillance duties.

Mouse had recently made the mistake of damaging data that showed a girl visiting Tatsuya at his villa. The incident had been deemed a result of a machine malfunction, and Mouse himself had not been blamed. However, for someone who had survived in the world of intelligence for over a decade, it was all very frustrating.

Mouse had successfully captured images of the girl's face, but he couldn't perform a skeletal match with nothing more than an illustrated portrait to work with. To this day, the identity of the seemingly innocent, somewhat frumpy beauty remained unknown.

Mouse's current mission felt like a chance to redeem himself. He wanted nothing more than to continue tailing the targets until their destination was confirmed. But orders were orders. He left the shadows to join the main unit as instructed. Little did he know something had been watching him from above.

Across the Izu Peninsula, several golf courses had been converted into antiaircraft zones during the Great War. Although they were supposed to have been returned to their original owners once the war was over, some of them had been discarded because of the high costs of redevelopment and low anticipated revenue. These golf courses had become state-owned land for a government-instituted fee. However, even the state had neglected the areas after removing all traces of their antiaircraft weapons.

Tatsuya led Katsuto to one of these abandoned golf courses. He stopped and turned to face his older opponent.

"We won't have to worry about damaging the villa here."

"Are you sure you want to fight in such an open area?" Katsuto challenged, implying Tatsuya wouldn't stand a chance here.

"What? Are you afraid you might lose?" Tatsuya challenged back.

It was a cliché thing to say, but it seemed to work on his opponent.

"Fine," Katsuto said, immediately deploying a magical barrier. "You can go first."

This time, he was provoking Tatsuya to break through his defenses. In response, Tatsuya chose to put an end to their conversation. Almost like a magic trick, a handgun-shaped CAD suddenly appeared in his right hand.

Tatsuya aimed the Silver Horn Custom Trident at Katsuto without a hint of hesitation. Multiple intense flashes sparked around the older boy. These were not lights visible to the naked eye, but everyone present here was more than capable of sensing them. They could all recognize the sparks of psion light. There were a total of eighteen flashes, but not a single attack hit Katsuto's body.

"Is that an Area-Interference Information-Boosting Psion Wall sequence?" Tatsuya mused in an attempt to unsettle his opponent.

"I'm impressed you could tell," Katsuto smirked. "Unfortunately, defeating me will take a lot more than identifying my move."

Seeing Katsuto was unfazed, Tatsuya unleashed his disintegration magic once more. As its name suggested, Psion Wall was a spell that formed a wall around its caster by solidifying psions into a high-density material. It may look like a defensive version of Program

Demolition, but unlike Tomitsuka's innate defense, Psion Wall was formed during the psion solidification process. This meant Tatsuya's magic could break it down. The problem was that right after destroying the Psion Wall, a powerful Area Interference dome emerged. Every time Tatsuya shattered a Psion Wall, it revealed an Information Boost shield. Once that broke, Juumonji simply cast Psion Wall again. Then there was a round of Area Interference just when you may think it was an Information Boost, followed by another Area Interference. It went Psion Wall, Information Boost, Area Interference. Then Psion Wall, Psion Wall, Area Interference, and Information Boost in an endless cycle of defense magic.

The spells weren't deployed simultaneously, so they couldn't all be eradicated at once. Due to this lack of regularity, Tatsuya couldn't predetermine and destroy several layers in one shot. His ability wasn't limited to magic programs or psionic information bodies. He could recognize any simple object with similar properties as a set and apply dispersion magic to multiple elements rather than one element at a time.

The main issue at hand was that Katsuto's magical barrier triggered the collapse of the deployed barriers and created new barriers in rapid succession. This made it so Tatsuya, despite his special ability, couldn't break the main structure producing the barriers. Each time the structure was shattered, a new one was generated. If this continued at a speed that matched Tatsuya's, his dispersion spell would fall behind.

Ultimately, Tatsuya's magic was overwhelmingly ineffective against Katsuto's defensive Phalanx. To break through the deadlock, Tatsuya temporarily paused his attacks. Suddenly, a two-dimensional wall surged toward him. This was the offensive Phalanx, which relentlessly crushed its target with an impenetrable wall. Tatsuya could work with this since the spell had already been activated in the physical realm and there was no magic program Tatsuya couldn't dispel. In a single blow, he shattered the twenty-four-layer magical barrier.

"Interesting," Katsuto said, smirking in admiration.

He knew the offensive Phalanx was completely incompatible with Tatsuya's magic, and yet he showed no sign of panic. He crouched down. Tatsuya's Elemental Sight revealed Katsuto's magic-calculation region was emitting intense psion light. Clearly, Katsuto had excessively activated his magic-calculation region, much like Ichijou clan head Gouki Ichijou had a month ago.

Here he comes! Tatsuya thought, preparing himself.

Katsuto's massive form soared through the air. In addition to a defensive barrier, he deployed a spherical anti-matter barrier, turning himself into a forward-charging projectile. Tatsuya extended his left hand to unleash a high-pressure psionic wave—Program Demolition.

Just then, Katsuto's anti-matter barrier vanished. Tatsuya's spell penetrated through Area Interference and dispelled his opponent's movement magic. However, while Katsuto was still in midair, he reactivated his movement magic and anti-matter barrier. Or rather, he created a new barrier inches from an impending collision.

Just before impact, Tatsuya successfully shattered the anti-matter barrier again. But he couldn't neutralize the movement magic. Katsuto tackle-rammed powerfully into Tatsuya's shoulder.

"Tatsuya!" Minami screamed from the sidelines.

The younger boy was sent flying and landed on a patch of ground covered with weeds. Miyuki simply pursed her lips as she gazed on intently.

Rolling himself over while simultaneously using flash casting, Tatsuya created distance between himself and Katsuto. The older boy didn't immediately press the advantage. It seemed his goal was not to destroy Tatsuya but simply subdue him.

"Using reinforcement magic now, are we?" Tatsuya muttered as he stood up.

He realized Katsuto had been able to hit him so powerfully by activating reinforcement magic on the shoulder of his jacket.

"Is there a reason I shouldn't use it?" Katsuto scoffed.

Once again, he emitted a surplus of psion light. Tatsuya knew his opponent was overheating his magic-calculation region on purpose. It was the Juumonji trump card, Overclock. This was a technique that deliberately overworked the magic-calculation region to reach beyond the caster's own potential and temporarily increase his magic's power. Essentially, it ensured victory at the cost of the caster's lifespan. It was a curse referred to as the capital's final wall of defense, where defeat was unforgivable.

Katsuto's father and former head of the Juumonji family, Kazuki, had even lost his magic from the repeated use of Overclock. Katsuto had witnessed that firsthand. Yet here he was using the technique against Tatsuya.

Tatsuya quickly dispelled Katsuto's anti-physical barrier as the older boy zipped forward, a few inches off the ground. Then he dodged a tackle by stepping to the side. But before they could completely pass each other, Katsuto's anti-physical barrier suddenly expanded.

Once again, Tatsuya was sent flying. As he tumbled across the grass, Katsuto closed in. His right foot came down, and his anti-physical barrier molded to the shape of his sole.

Tatsuya narrowly avoided being crushed under Katsuto's foot. But as he rose to his feet, Katsuto thrust out his fist. At ultraclose quarters, he released an offensive Phalanx. Tatsuya used his ability to disperse it. However, right behind that fist, another one approached, shrouded in anti-physical barriers and Area Interference.

Tatsuya's arm, which had blocked the punch, bent in an unnatural direction. He jumped backward to mitigate the punch's force. By the time his feet touched the ground, there seemed to be no sign of broken bones. However, once he landed, he lost all leverage for a jump. If only he had a fraction of a second more, he might have avoided the attack. But Katsuto didn't allow him even the tiniest bit of breathing room.

Katsuto tackled Tatsuya in the shoulder once again, sending the younger boy flying nearly ten meters. If he had collided with a car, the damage wouldn't have been so bad. Tatsuya felt as if he had been struck by a large truck. He lay sprawled on the ground.

He coughed up blood, which splattered on the ground. Clearly, he had sustained significant internal injuries.

"Tatsuya!"

This time, it was Mayumi who called his name. Miyuki tightly clutched her hands against her chest, enduring the worry in silence with her eyes fixed on Tatsuya. Katsuto reached out his right hand, preparing to cast another spell.

"Enough already!" Mari yelled.

But Katsuto ignored her and unleashed an offensive Phalanx at Tatsuya, who was still collapsed on the ground. A two-dimensional barrier capable of crushing an armored vehicle flew Tatsuya's way. But its thirty-two layers suddenly vanished before making contact.

"What the...?" Katsuto gasped in confusion.

He had thought Tatsuya was no longer capable of fighting back. But the younger boy's arms twitched before slowly pressing against the ground to lift up his upper body. Little by little, he rose to his feet. Not only were there no traces of blood around his mouth, but the bloodstains on the ground had also disappeared.

"Is this your Regenerate spell?" Katsuto said with obvious surprise. But he quickly pulled himself together and cast another defensive Phalanx.

Tatsuya didn't say a word, his face devoid of any emotion. In fact, his entire humanity seemed to have disappeared. He extended his left arm toward Katsuto, his handgun-shaped CAD gripped in his fist. This CAD was slightly different from the object that dangled limply from his lowered right hand. Attached to its tip—the gun barrel— was what looked like a fifteen-centimeter-long metallic stake.

Getting a bad feeling, Katsuto hesitated to move forward. Instead of advancing straight ahead, he attempted to dodge sidewise. But Tatsuya was quicker to pull the trigger. No one saw what happened next. All that was clear was that some kind of magic had been cast.

* * *

"Argh…" Katsuto groaned, falling to his knees.

"Juumonji!" Mayumi shrieked.

"Are you okay?!" Mari echoed.

Using his right arm to grip his left, Katsuto realized his left arm had carbonized at the elbow. Everything below that had fallen to the ground.

"What did you…do?" Katsuto winced.

He didn't need an answer from Tatsuya to know what had happened. But he had to know what had pierced through his barrier.

Tatsuya replied anyway: "Baryon Lance. Lancehead is an interpersonal spell that disintegrates into electrons, protons, and neutrons. It then absorbs electrons into protons and emits neutron radiation."

"So it's a neutron cannon?" Katsuto said in disbelief while gritting his teeth in pain. "Radiation-contaminating weapons like that are prohibited by the International Magic Association!"

"But there is no radiation contamination," Tatsuya responded calmly. "No radioactive residue is left behind. You can still tell there was an attack, but all neutrons are reverted back to where they came from."

"Through Regenerate?" Katsuo asked.

"That's right."

Tatsuya aimed Lancehead at Katsuto once more. This time at his heart.

"Surrender, Juumonji."

"……" Katsuto scowled in silence.

"Your Phalanx can't stop my Baryon Lance," Tatsuya advised. "But you should know that already."

"Juumonji!" Mayumi yelled, manipulating her CAD. But her activation sequence froze before she could cast.

"Is this your doing, Miyuki?!" she said, glaring angrily.

"Yes," Miyuki replied calmly and quietly. "I cast the anti-magic Freeze Program. You cannot use your CAD, Saegusa."

"Then I'll take another route!" Mayumi said defiantly.

CADs were essential tools for current-day magicians, but they were not mandatory for casting spells. Modern magic, after all, had evolved from psychic abilities that could bend reality with a single thought. Powerful enough magicians could cast spells without a CAD, especially if they were adept at a particular type of magic. The only downsides were that it took longer to cast without a CAD and an incantation was needed to prompt the construction of the magic program within the magic-calculation region.

"Set: Entropy Reduction, Density Manipulation, Phase Transition, Coagulation, Energy Form Transformation, Acceleration, Sublimation— Entry! Execute event modification! Spell name: Dry Meteor!"

This was the type of incantation used in the modern magic system. Although it came out essentially as a mix of English and Japanese words, the spoken language itself didn't matter. As long as the magician verbalized the concepts clearly to themselves, there was actually no need to say it aloud. Performing it in front of an enemy, however, left the magician vulnerable during the time it took to cast.

This was why modern magic had abandoned verbal incantations and chosen to use CADs instead. As Mayumi chanted the spell, Miyuki did not launch an attack. There was no need. Mayumi's Dry Meteor never activated.

"Is this the power of Area Interference?" Mayumi gasped.

"I will not let anyone interfere with Tatsuya's fight," Miyuki declared.

Mari kicked the ground in silence. She held a dagger in her hand that she had concealed this whole time. If magic was off the table, she would just have to use a physical weapon against Miyuki. This would have been a solid idea if Miyuki had been alone. Or if Minami were the ordinary girl she appeared to be. However, Minami didn't miss a beat and raised a pistol to Mari's head before the older girl could even move.

"Miss Watanabe, I would appreciate it if you put away your

weapon," Minami said, maintaining her usual politeness despite the situation.

Mari gritted her teeth in frustration.

Pistols posed a threat to non-magicians and magicians alike, especially in situations like this where magic wasn't an option due to Miyuki's Area Interference. Minami seemed to know how to handle a gun, so there was no room for resistance.

Mari didn't dare accuse Minami of foul play. It was her own fault she had only prepared a dagger while her junior had concealed a gun. Mari had to admit she had been too naive. Avoiding that fact went against her sense of pride. To compensate, she yelled a few words of encouragement to her teammate.

"Juumonji! Despite Tatsuya's fancy weapon, he's ultimately just attacking with neutron radiation! Neutron Barrier should be able to block it!"

Despite Mari's support, Katsuto remained on his knees.

"Sorry to break it to you, but Neutron Barrier doesn't stand a chance against my Baryon Lance," Tatsuya said.

"What?!" Mari gasped.

"Don't listen to what he says, Juumonji!" Mayumi chimed in. "Neutron Barrier is a perfected technique. It can definitely block neutron radiation!"

"That's exactly why it doesn't work," Tatsuya said cryptically.

At least, he sounded cryptic to Mayumi and Mari. Katsuto understood exactly what Tatsuya meant.

Neutron radiation had high piercing abilities. The properties of matter directly interfered with events through information. It was difficult to block high-piercing, information-based neutron radiation with magic, because it was defined as a property that was difficult to block.

However, the primary goal of modern magic since the very beginning had been to prevent disasters caused by nuclear fission. Blocking neutron radiation was a theme modern magic couldn't easily avoid. In fact, numerous researchers had been devoted to finding ways to block neutron radiation with magic. The results of their tireless work had been the creation of Neutron Barrier.

This spell had been perfected only to block neutron radiation. When it was ever at play, Neutron Barrier became the go-to spell for magicians. It was the only completely effective magic that stood a chance.

Once they had perfected this spell, magic researchers hadn't bothered exploring other methods. There were no successful instances of blocking neutron radiation with alternative techniques, even by the Juumonji family magicians.

Neutron Barrier was the only magical barrier that could block neutron radiation. Not even Phalanx stood a chance. However, if he knew what spell was being used in advance, there was no type of magic Tatsuya couldn't break down. His Baryon Lance was capable of converting Lancehead into neutron radiation for projection, reconstructing Lancehead, and breaking down Neutron Barrier.

Even if Katsuto cast Area Interference, the results would be the same, since neutralizing Area Interference would simultaneously break down Neutron Barrier. And in that fleeting moment when both defense systems were down, Tatsuya's neutron radiation would reach his target.

Katsuto could have deployed Neutron Barrier earlier, but Phalanx could handle almost any attack. It could block high-speed massive bodies, liquid dispersion, gas permeation, sound waves, electromagnetic waves, gravitational waves, psionic waves, and more. It even had a barrier against neutron radiation. But Tatsuya's Baryon Lance had pierced through its defense. Both parties knew repeating the same casting sequence would simply yield the same result.

"I've lost," Katsuto said.

"No!" Mayumi shrieked.

"Juumonji!" Mari echoed.

Katsuto stood up, raising his remaining right hand into the air as a sign of defeat.

The information officer who went by the codename Monkey had been monitoring the intense battle through a pair of binoculars. The outcome came as a shock to say the least. The Intelligence Department had predicted Katsuto would emerge victorious in the clash between the two young men. They had even planned to abduct the weakened Tatsuya after his defeat.

Monkey quickly turned on his communication device. He had kept it off to avoid detection if he received any communications. The purely optical binoculars were probably too outdated to be detected, but it was better to be safe than sorry.

Even after turning on the device, Monkey refrained from any careless actions that might involve transmitting audio. He simply sent the prearranged signal. A response came right away, signaling for a strong offensive strategy.

Deep down, Monkey wanted to retreat. While he, too, was a magician, witnessing Katsuto and Tatsuya's battle had significantly dampened his morale. Clearly, Tatsuya's skills were leagues beyond what the Intelligence Department could handle. Monkey belonged specifically to the Special Affairs Section. Although it was part of the same Intelligence Department, this division didn't place as much trust in Tsukasa Tooyama's magic as Counterintelligence did. Monkey, for one, did not believe the magic of Tooyama—a family outside the Ten Master Clans—could stand up against a Yotsuba magician's.

Then again, orders were orders. Monkey stood up from his crouched position to rejoin the main unit. He consoled himself by thinking this was better than being ordered to shoot at the "monster" himself. Suddenly, a flood of colors overwhelmed his eyes. It was as if he were undergoing a color vision test. Particles of light bearing every imaginable color danced and swirled together, filling his entire field of vision. In an effort to escape the madness-inducing light, his consciousness plummeted into darkness.

Tatsuya and Katsuto faced each other, Katsuto's left arm as good as new thanks to Tatsuya's Regenerate.

"So, Shiba," the older boy asked. "What do you want from me now?"

"I want you to go back empty-handed and make sure no one tries to have this conversation with me again," Tatsuya said simply.

"That's fair," Katsuto said with a shrug. He had no right to decline the victor's request. But he couldn't help but add one thing. "As I said before, the situation is only getting worse, and we can't avoid it any longer. The Magic Association may risk displeasing the Yotsuba family to expose you as Taurus Silver. But even if they don't, the public will eventually force you to participate in the project."

Tatsuya remained silent. He knew Katsuto wasn't trying to convince him of anything this time.

"Then if you refuse, there will be no place for you in the Japanese magical community, let alone in this country," the older boy continued. "At that point, not even Maya will be able to protect you anymore."

"No matter what happens, I will never join the Dione Project," Tatsuya said firmly.

"Why not?!" Mayumi shrieked in utter disbelief. "Why are you being so stubborn? It's not like the USNA wants to turn you into a lab rat or exploit you for labor. You'll be joining the project team as an honorable representative of Japan. The project itself even aims to solve the difficulties that face the future of humankind. You shouldn't risk isolating yourself from our entire nation just to avoid joining that cause!"

"The benefits of using magic for peaceful purposes should be enjoyed by magicians themselves," Tatsuya replied with the same firm tone he'd used with Katsuto.

This made Mayumi falter and fall silent.

"What do you mean?" Mari asked in her place.

"As I said before, the Dione Project has an ulterior motive," Tatsuya explained.

"And what is that?" Mari insisted.

"To expel all problematic magicians from the face of the Earth," Tatsuya stated.

"Th-that's ridiculous. What are you saying?" Mayumi interjected in a whirlwind of emotions and confusion.

"I'm saying the more I think about the Dione Project, the more convinced I am that its primary motive is to accomplish hidden agendas," Tatsuya explained.

"Tell me more," Katsuto said with a serious expression.

Tatsuya was more than happy to oblige.

"In its execution phase," he began, "the Dione Project requires the deployment of numerous magicians to Venus's satellite orbit, the asteroid belt, Jupiter's atmosphere, and Jupiter's moon Ganymede. Considering the current state of space-travel technology, once someone joins the team, they won't be able to return to Earth for any extended period. Even if they put magicians on rotations, as soon as someone's rehabilitation on Earth is over, they'll be sent back to the field."

"That can't be true," Mayumi insisted.

"The number of magicians who meet the necessary conditions for the project is incredibly low compared with how many are actually required," Tatsuya countered. "In other words, magicians deployed in the execution phase are essentially being sacrificed for the future of humanity. Using magicians as tools in outer space mirrors the current situation on Earth where we serve as weapons and expendable assets. Sorry to disappoint you, but the Dione Project won't affect any real change."

Upon receiving a report from the Special Affairs Section, which had been monitoring Tatsuya and Katsuto's battle, the Intelligence Department's Tatsuya Abduction Unit was on the move. Tsukasa Tooyama was one of its members. She was shocked by Katsuto's defeat, but she didn't let it show on her face.

Tsukasa's intuition told her to abort the mission and retreat. Unfortunately, this operation was being led by the Intelligence Department's deputy director. She didn't have the authority to make any cancellations.

It doesn't seem like Katsuto has completely lost his ability to fight, Tsukasa reassured herself. *And I'm sure the Saegusa girl would support us if needed.*

She and her team members stealthily advanced across the area to avoid making any noise. They were headed to the abandoned golf course where Tatsuya was. Rather than take the road leading straight to it, they approached from the shadows of the surrounding mountain range. Once they passed this area, they would be able to spot the target and the battle would begin. Along the way, they encountered a densely wooded slope.

Suddenly, a flood of chaotic colors appeared before the unit's eyes. The seemingly random and flickering light particles depicted a color pattern that induced sleep in humans. Half the assault team fell unconscious. The remaining half managed to cancel out the light magic and narrowly escape falling under the hypnotic spell thanks to the individual magical barriers Tsukasa quickly put into place.

The second lieutenant commanding the unit repeatedly shouted to everyone to fall back into formation. But out of the over thirty troops, less than twenty were still awake. Of the three squad leaders, only one was standing. The breakdown in the chain of command had thrown the unit into confusion and disarray.

It was the perfect opportunity to attack. A small, female figure rushed down the slope. In fact, she wasn't that small. She was the average height for a girl. Once she made it to the front lines, she slipped through the tree branches and swung down a glimmering weapon—a katana. Its blade collided with one of the individual shields Tsukasa had cast. Although the soldier within the shield shouldn't have been struck directly, he staggered and collapsed.

It's that hypnotic magic again! Tsukasa realized.

The second the shield shifted into defense mode, the light magic that had put half the troops to sleep struck again. Tsukasa couldn't hide her shock at falling prey to this tactic. The second lieutenant, however, failed to comprehend what was going on. Ironically, his lack of awareness didn't impede his decision-making.

"Fire!" he shouted.

All assault rifles were instantly trained on the girl. However, before any of them could be fired, a large male figure shielded the girl with his frame. A series of gunshots echoed through the air. Most of the bullets hit the young man's body, but he didn't fall to the ground or even bleed. The bullets simply fell to his feet.

"High-powered rifle team!" the second lieutenant commanded, his voice verging on a scream.

Four soldiers armed with anti-magician weapons rushed to the front. Suddenly, thunder boomed. But it wasn't the sound of the high-powered rifles or real lightning. Only the deafening noise reverberated through the air.

Tsukasa's individual shields were designed to withstand sonic attacks, so none of the soldiers were hurt or disoriented by the thunderous noise. What the noise did do was disrupt the commander's orders. The high-powered rifle team remained in place, but inactive.

The thunder didn't stop after one rumble. Like the drumming of a thunder god, it shook the air repeatedly, sending tremors into the soldiers themselves. As a result, they failed to realize it wasn't just the air that was shaking.

Suddenly, the earth split open, with fissures running in all directions. Exposed tree roots made the trees tilt dangerously toward the ground. The cracks weren't that deep, but they were big enough to disturb the soldiers.

"Pull back! Out of the forest!" the second lieutenant ordered.

At that moment, the thundering abruptly ceased. The Intelligence Department rarely engaged in group combat outdoors. Their field of expertise was usually limited to urban areas. So even cases involving gunfire typically occurred individually or in small groups. Their sudden retreat in this natural setting was understandably far from orderly. Many of their feet became entangled in the underbrush, making them stumble and fall. It must have felt as if the grass had come to life and reached out to ensnare them.

Amid the chaos, Tsukasa tried to get a grasp on the situation. At this point, she had a grasp of the positions of her team members who had retreated on two legs but had lost track of anyone who had fallen. As soon as they had disappeared from her awareness, the individual shields she had placed on them had also vanished.

Just then, a cascade of lightning showered down upon the unit even though they were in a dense forest. But the lightning didn't come from the sky. It shot through the gaps between the trees, shocking any soldier who remained in the wooded area.

The soldiers who emerged from the forest met a slightly better fate, though one could argue that was worse. Riot-control nets rained down from above, ensuring none of the soldiers escaped.

At this point, Tsukasa was the only one still standing. She bit her lip at the sight of her comrades falling victim to shocks or capture. Her individual shield could block bullets, bombs, and even poison gas. But it didn't grant superhuman physical abilities to those it was protecting. Once the shield was ensnared in a net, escape and resistance became impossible. Tsukasa had never thought riot-control projectiles would become the bane of her magic.

"It looks like you're the only one left."

The speaker was a young swordswoman, Erika Chiba, who grasped a blade in her hand. Tsukasa was well aware Erika was closing in on her and her escape route had been blocked.

"Are you Erika Chiba?" she asked.

"That's right," Erika replied plainly, without the witty remark Tsukasa had anticipated.

"I'm National Defense Force Sergeant Major Tsukasa Tooyama," Tsukasa explained.

"Okay," Erika said, seemingly uninterested. Tsukasa wasn't sure if this was an act or how she truly felt.

"For your information, we were in the middle of a mission," she said sharply, taking the offensive despite the katana in Erika's hand.

"Yeah, and?"

"Impeding a military mission can lead to charges of assault, injury, obstruction of official duties, and violation of the Firearms and Swords Control Law, just to name a few."

Erika kept an eye on Tsukasa and let out a deep sigh.

"You guys really ought to learn," she said, showing no sign of backing down.

"What do you mean?" Tsukasa asked.

"Even National Defense Force soldiers need permission to carry weapons outside designated areas or exercises," Erika stated, her gaze unwavering. "Those firearms you guys are carrying require a lot of paperwork, which you have definitely not submitted. Sorry to break it to you, but the ones in violation of the Firearms and Swords Control Law are you."

"You sure know a lot for a high schooler," Tsukasa remarked.

Erika ignored this and continued, "This isn't the first time I've caught you swinging weapons around without permission under the guise of 'training.' That really puts the police in a bad mood."

"How would you know?" Tsukasa countered. "You're not a police officer."

"No, but I have a whole group of them waiting outside this forest. Don't play dumb with me." Erika sighed in exasperation, lowering her weapon. But this didn't mean she had let her guard down.

"The police can seek support from civilian magicians to address magic crimes," she continued. "Any magician should know about that exception."

Tsukasa smiled an emotionless smile.

"Anyhow," Erika said. "I'd appreciate it if you came along with me and accepted the consequences quietly. I'm sure you don't want things to get ugly."

The moment she finished speaking, Tsukasa wrapped herself in a magic shield. Then, without a moment's delay, she cast a movement spell on herself.

Unfazed, Erika calmly sidestepped Tsukasa's flying form and swept her katana horizontally through the air, resulting in a loud crack. Erika's attack colliding with Tsukasa's shield had proved too much for the blade, and it had snapped in half. Tsukasa continued her escape into the mountains. But before she could proceed, Leo stood in her way. As Tsukasa assumed a shoulder-tackle stance in midair, Leo planted his feet into the ground, prepared to counter. Tsukasa's shield collided with Leo's body, but the young man didn't budge.

Tsukasa, on the other hand, flew backward, and her movement spell dissipated. Erika approached her with smooth and stable steps, seemingly unaffected by the rough terrain filled with cracks and exposed tree roots. Her straight posture suggested she was even walking on paved road. Tsukasa felt she was trapped on all sides.

All she could do was protect herself with her shield. To ensure she could move at any moment and avoid obstacles as needed, she reconstructed her shield to form-fit her body. Erika swung her broken blade. It didn't hit Tsukasa, or even her shield. Erika had misjudged the distance now that her katana was half its original length.

Tsukasa saw an opportunity in this unlikely stroke of luck. Erika remained in a stance, preparing to strike. To Tsukasa, it appeared as if Erika was frozen. Seeing this as her chance to escape, she stepped forward with her right foot. Just as she did this, her knee buckled and her leg went limp. Her left leg also lacked the strength to walk. In fact, her whole body had gone limp, forcing her to crumple to the ground.

Erika finally released her stance. Tsukasa looked up at her. It was only then that she noticed the psion blade, shimmering like a heat wave at the end of Erika's broken weapon. The heat wave blade disappeared.

"Ethereal Hidden Sword Technique, *Kirikage*," Erika whispered.

That was the last thing Tsukasa heard before falling unconscious.

"Using magicians as tools in outer space mirrors the current situation on Earth where we serve as weapons and expendable assets. Sorry to disappoint you, but the Dione Project won't affect any real change. And I can't accept that."

Tatsuya's statement took Katsuto, Mayumi, and Mari by surprise. They finally realized he hadn't been refusing the invitation to join the project without good reason.

"But, Tatsuya!" Mayumi interjected.

She understood Tatsuya's determination and conviction. That was precisely why she couldn't help but raise her voice with tears in her eyes.

"Even if your prediction is right," she sobbed, "you're still going to lose your place in this country if you insist on refusing to join the project. You're still going to end up suffering alone!"

She couldn't bear to see him end up as a sacrifice. Even if it meant deceiving the entire world, pretending to comply might ultimately be Tatsuya's best choice.

"Tatsuya won't ever be alone," a voice from the woods interrupted.

Tatsuya and Katsuto were on the main terrain of the abandoned golf course, what was formerly the first hole. A mountain range surged on their right. No longer maintained, it was now overgrown with scraggly vegetation. A group of four familiar people descended from these mountains. It was Erika, Leo, Mikihiko, and Honoka. Although not currently within range, Mitsuki and Shizuku were also probably nearby.

"We'll be with him," Leo claimed, lugging a woman on his shoulders.

Katsuto frowned as he recognized her.

"I think you know this woman, Juumonji," Leo said, fearlessly laying Tsukasa at Katsuto's feet. "Mind taking her with you?"

"A-anyway, we won't leave Tatsuya alone!" Honoka stammered nervously but bravely.

"That's right," Mikihiko chimed in. "Tatsuya is our friend. No, he's more than that. We owe him a debt we can never repay. Even if the world brands him as a criminal, we would never abandon him."

"What does owing him have to do with anything? He's our friend and that's all that matters," Leo said, wrapping his arm around Mikihiko's shoulders.

Katsuto lifted Tsukasa from the ground and turned to Tatsuya.

"You have great friends, Shiba," he said. "It almost makes me jealous."

With that, he turned his back on the group and walked back toward his SUV parked in the villa driveway.

"Wait for me, Juumonji!" Mayumi called, running after him.

"I guess we really lost this one." Mari shrugged and followed Mayumi.

With a drained complexion, Tatsuya gazed at his unexpected visitors. They all had bashful smiles on their faces. Only Erika averted her gaze, but she was clearly smiling, too. Tatsuya then turned to Miyuki, who was wiping away tears.

[10]

On Monday morning, Tatsuya found himself alone in his Izu villa. He had sent Miyuki back to her new flat in Chofu during the early evening of the day before. This morning, he was eating a breakfast Pixie had prepared while watching the news on TV. At least, he claimed to be watching it. In reality, it was only playing in the background.

Apart from the day before when he had sat with Miyuki at the table, mornings were generally uneventful. This morning's breakfast was supposed to be the same. However, something on TV caused everything to change.

"Breaking news!" the announcer declared. His frantic voice caught Tatsuya's attention.

"First, take a look at this message."

The camera shifted to a large monitor next to the announcer. The blue screen suddenly switched to a bust shot of a suspicious-looking figure. At first glance, it was impossible to tell whether they were a man or a woman. Their age and race lay shrouded in mystery as well.

The individual was draped in a gray, hooded robe, which entirely covered their body. Their face was concealed behind a mask of white resin. The television speakers relayed the mystery person's voice, emitted by the monitor.

"Greetings. I am one of the Seven Sages. The First Sage, to be precise."

The voice was electronically processed, making it impossible to reproduce the original sound, even with advanced computer technology. Though, from the tone, the mystery person appeared to be male.

"I have a secret to reveal to all the citizens of Japan," they announced.

While their Japanese was fluent, their manner of speaking made Tatsuya suspect this person might not be Japanese. As he pondered who it could be, the term "Seven Sages" brought to mind the face of a certain boy. It was the boy from the heat of the Vampire Incident who had sent a video message. If Tatsuya remembered correctly, the name of this boy, who was also an acquaintance of Shizuku's from her time abroad, was Raymond Clark.

Clark? Tatsuya thought. The family name rang a bell, but he decided to focus on the news for now.

"It is my greatest hope that the USNA's Dione Project is swiftly put into action," the mystery person stated. *"To achieve that, we desperately need participation from Japan, specifically from Taurus Silver."*

Tatsuya had now connected three individuals in his mind: Edward Clark, Raymond Clark, and this mystery person.

"I repeat," the mystery person declared. *"We need Taurus Silver, also known as Tatsuya Shiba."*

At this point, there was no doubt in Tatsuya's mind. This mysterious figure who went by *the First Sage* was Raymond Clark, and Raymond Clark was Edward Clark's son.

"Taurus Silver is Tatsuya Shiba, a current senior at the National Magic University Affiliated First High School. Citizens of Japan, I ask of you to convince Tatsuya to join our cause."

The video message ended there.

From Tatsuya's point of view, Raymond Clark's intervention had come completely out of left field. In fact, he had not expected anything like it.

Tatsuya had prepared countermeasures for scenarios where the Magic Association exposed Taurus Silver's identity or where the government applied pressure. He had also arranged measures for dealing with Edward Clark if he ever grew impatient waiting for Tatsuya's response. However, none of the strategies he had come up with could deal with something like this. Tatsuya realized he had been backed into a corner.

(To be continued in the Escape Arc, Part I)

AFTERWORD

You have just finished reading Volume 23, *Isolation Arc*. Did you enjoy it?

I have been wanting to write this arc since this series first began. Its title was conceived after starting this volume, but the framework leading to the climax has remained unchanged since before my debut. My tendency to state that Katsuto is currently the strongest character was also something I did with this arc's confrontation in mind. Tatsuya's new spell, Baryon Lance, was a special tool I prepared for this book. You won't believe how invested I was in this arc. I felt an immense sense of relief when I typed "To be continued" at the end. I had finally written the story that had been in my mind for ages.

That doesn't mean my writing process was smooth. Although I had been steadily preparing the groundwork leading up to Tatsuya and Katsuto's showdown, there were still various aspects that needed adjustment. For example, Fumiya's cross-dressing scene was something I added abruptly when I realized his face had been revealed during the Nine School Competition. Not to say unexpected additions like that can't be fun.

The *Isolation Arc* undoubtedly has one of the biggest climaxes in *The Irregular at Magic High School* series. But it's not the biggest one there will ever be. This arc's confrontation is more a conflict among friends; the true enemy is lurking elsewhere. I'm sure some readers can guess who the final boss may be. But be warned—there's at least one more twist to come. The story is already heating up.

In this volume, I emphasized the narrative flow and intentionally refrained from delving into behind-the-scenes details or meticulous elements. While I feel this aligns with the nature of storytelling in novels, I also recognize sometimes I may have left out too much information. To compensate, I'll briefly supplement what was omitted in the main story here. I know some readers don't like reading about additional details, so I'll wrap up the afterword and put the additions on the following page.

I also introduced the fictional Venus development venture known as the Dione Project in this volume. To help me with this part of the story, I received invaluable insights from Dr. Naoyuki Higo of the Japan Aerospace Exploration Agency, Ms. Naoko Sakurai of the Japan Space Forum, and science writer Isana Kashiwai. It was also novelist Taiyo Fujii who facilitated my meeting with Mr. Kashiwai. I'd like to take this opportunity to extend my warm thanks to all of them.

I'm writing this afterword just before the release of the *Irregular* film. I haven't seen the advance screening yet, so I can only write about the film based on the information I received during production. However, I know it will be an interesting and compelling addition to the franchise, suited for the big screen.

The subtitle of the next volume will be the *Escape Arc*, and it will probably be Part I. In terms of my schedule, I will be working on the novelization of the film first. I plan to write an unabridged version that includes episodes that had to be cut for the theatrical release.

The exact format I will be delivering it to you in, however, has not been decided yet. Once things are certain, I'll be sure to make an announcement.

Until then, I hope to see you again in my next work, whether that be the *Escape Arc* or the uncut edition of *The Girl Who Summons the Stars*.

Tsutomu Sato

Supplementary (or Useless Additional) Material

○ *Kirikage*

This is Erika's Ethereal Hidden Sword Technique. It made its first appearance in the anime film *The Girl Who Summons the Stars*. I then imported this new typeless magic originally created for the film back into the novel. The technique forms a magic sword that causes damage to the psion body of another. With a single slash, it deprives an opponent of all their motor functions.

Since the attack's target—the psionic information body—is not linked strongly with the eidos of the physical body, it naturally forms an afterimage-like form that overlaps with the physical body in the material world. Advanced martial artists can (hypothetically) control their physical bodies by moving this afterimage in advance. *Kirikage* takes advantage of this principle in reverse by literally cutting through shadows to disrupt the control over one's physical body.

This technique is an offensive method against information bodies that Erika forced herself to learn after realizing she did not have an effective attack against the parasites during the *Visitor Arc*. Originally, only Jouichirou Chiba, the head of the Chiba family, could use this secret move. But Erika managed to master it without direct guidance from her father by researching secret scrolls.

○ *The spell that puts the Intelligence Department unit to sleep*

The mysterious light that lulled the Intelligence Department team to sleep as they tried to attack Tatsuya through the forest was Honoka's spell Hypno Eye. This is an upgraded version of Evil Eye, which Honoka used to put the Intelligence Department to sleep in Volume 11, the *Visitor Arc*. In its improved state, the spell now has more power, greater target count, and wider range.

○ *The fissures and lightning that attacked the Intelligence Department unit*

This was the spell that Mikihiko used against the new Monolith Code opponent, Kichijouji. It's a combination of Rumbling, Fissure, Disheveled Hair, and Antlion Pit.

○ *Why Erika and the others conveniently attacked the Intelligence Department unit*

You may ask, why were Erika and the others conveniently there to attack Tsukasa and her team? There was actually a conversation in the Izu villa living room after Katsuto, Mayumi, and Mari left that explains this, but it was omitted for the sake of the ending's pacing.

"By the way, Erika," Tatsuya began. "That's the SMAT you brought with you, isn't it?"

"Yeah," Erika responded nonchalantly. "Why do you ask?"

"That can't be a coincidence," Tatsuya insisted. "How did you know the National Defense Force was going to be here today?"

"I had no idea they were going to be here," Erika said with a shrug. "All I knew was something big was going to happen. Miyuki gave it all away with her strange behavior."

"I did?" Miyuki asked.

"Remember when you told us not to visit Tatsuya because Juumonji was visiting on Sunday?" she reminded.

"Y-yes."

"You didn't need to tell us he'd be visiting specifically. You could have just said Tatsuya would be busy. And yet you mentioned Juumonji—something which should have been a secret."

"Oh…"

"I acted chill about it back then, but I knew right away something was up. Worst-case scenario, an uninvited guest may even show up. That's when I did some digging."

So this was how Erika arrived in Izu with a special police unit of Chiba Dojo disciples.

That concludes the Supplementary (or Useless Additional) Material section. See you in the *Escape Arc*.

HAVE YOU BEEN TURNED ON TO LIGHT NOVELS YET?

86—EIGHTY-SIX, VOL. 1-12

In truth, there is no such thing as a bloodless war. Beyond the fortified walls protecting the eighty-five Republic Sectors lies the "nonexistent" Eighty-Sixth Sector. The young men and women of this forsaken land are branded the Eighty-Six and, stripped of their humanity, pilot "unmanned" weapons into battle...

Manga adaptation available now!

WOLF & PARCHMENT, VOL. 1-9

The young man Col dreams of one day joining the holy clergy and departs on a journey from the bathhouse, Spice and Wolf. Winfiel Kingdom's prince has invited him to help correct the sins of the Church. But as his travels begin, Col discovers in his luggage a young girl with a wolf's ears and tail named Myuri, who stowed away for the ride!

Manga adaptation available now!

SOLO LEVELING, VOL. 1-8

E-rank hunter Jinwoo Sung has no money, no talent, and no prospects to speak of—and apparently, no luck, either! When he enters a hidden double dungeon one fateful day, he's abandoned by his party and left to die at the hands of some of the most horrific monsters he's ever encountered.

Comic adaptation available now!

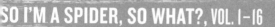